THE IRISHMAN

THE MAX JONES THRILLERS
BOOK 2

MARK DAVID ABBOTT

1

L iam Mulroney rubbed his face and glanced at Barry. The strain of the last few hours was evident in the lines around Barry's eyes and the tight, grim set of his jaw.

They had driven hard and fast for two hours along the E44, heading toward the Hatta border crossing into Oman.

The sun was just beginning to rise, casting soft rays that bathed the desert in hues of pink and gold, but Liam found no beauty in it. The rage that had burned inside him had long since faded, replaced by exhaustion as the adrenaline drained from his body.

"How are you feeling?"

"Alright," Barry replied with a grunt, his eyes focused on the road ahead.

"Do you want me to take over?"

"No," came the gruff reply.

Liam acknowledged him with a single nod and shifted in his seat. Images of the firefight and their escape from the villa flickered in his mind—the bodies of his dead men, the metallic scent of blood, the sound of bullets ricocheting off his prized vintage Aston Martin.

Oddly, he realized he felt more regret about the Aston Martin than about leaving his brother behind. But at least his brother could take care of himself and find a way out.

Besides, it served his brother right to face some difficulty in his otherwise cushy life. After all, this whole mess had been his brother's fault in the first place. Liam picked up his phone from the center console and glanced at the screen.

No messages.

Liam sniffed. His brother Caim should be safe by now. He had called the cops as soon as they fled the property, and he'd seen the patrol cars speed past as he and Barry drove off The Palm. They would have dealt with the shooter or shooters, whoever they were, and were probably giving Caim a hard time. Liam shrugged. He had no sympathy for his brother. Caim would face a few tough questions at first, but Colonel Hakim Al-Hamadi, his police contact, would sweep everything under the rug, and Caim would be released.

Liam chewed his lip. Still, it was odd that he hadn't heard from anyone yet.

He glanced at his phone again, frowning. He didn't want to be the first to reach out, but now that his anger had subsided, a bit of concern crept in.

Deciding to act, he tapped the screen, selected Caim's number, and dialed. Putting the phone on speaker, he waited as the call connected, only to frown when a robotic voice told him the phone was switched off. Liam ended the call and stared blankly out the windshield, his worry growing. After a moment, he selected another contact and dialed. The phone rang three times before the call was cut off.

Frowning deeper, he hit redial. This time, the call was cut immediately.

Grinding his teeth, he tossed the phone back into the centre console as Barry glanced over at him.

"Something wrong?" he asked.

"Caim's phone is turned off and Colonel Hakim is not taking my calls."

Barry said nothing, his eyes back on the road ahead.

Liam let out a frustrated sigh. In less than a week, everything he had built was crumbling around him. It had all started with his brother, but there was no point in continuing to blame him. His brother was an idiot, no doubt, but he was still family. Now, Liam had to focus on whoever was moving in on his territory and dismantling his business.

In just a few short days, ten of his most trusted men had been killed, and his house had been attacked. To make matters worse, his once-reliable police contact—the man he had paid hundreds of thousands of dirhams over the years —was now refusing to take his calls. Grinding his teeth, Liam tapped a nervous rhythm on his thigh with his forefinger, his frustration mounting.

Barry cleared his throat, then asked, "What do you want me to do?"

Liam's frown deepened, and he jabbed his finger at the highway ahead. "Just keep driving," he growled.

2

Colonel Hakim Al-Hamadi of the Dubai Police Force ignored the phone buzzing in his pocket and focused on the two bodies being wheeled toward him on gurneys by the paramedics. His mood was growing darker by the minute. He had been up since early morning, hadn't eaten breakfast, and hadn't even made it to the office yet. He hated anything that disrupted his routine.

What had initially seemed like a straightforward fire in a high-end villa on The Palm—a rare enough occurrence— had quickly spiraled into something worse. Now, he was staring at two bodies pulled from the neighboring property, both with their throats cut and found floating in the swimming pool of a house that had been vacant for the past six months.

He straightened his uniform and stepped forward, blocking the paramedic's path. The paramedic opened his mouth to protest but immediately fell silent and halted as soon as he saw Colonel Hakim's uniform.

Colonel Hakim drew himself to his full height and growled, "Unzip the bag."

The paramedic gulped and nodded. He walked to the front of the gurney and paused, his hand hovering over the zipper. "Sir, it's not a pleasant sight."

"Open it." Hakim repeated, and the paramedic unzipped the bag, exposing the head. Hakim frowned and stepped closer, turning so he could study the face. A European male, between thirty to forty years of age, his face puffy and white, the skin wrinkled from a lengthy submersion in the water. "Anyone we know?"

Major Omar Al Farsi shook his head. "Patrick Wilson, 32. British citizen. Ex British Army. Been here for three months on a tourist visa." He pointed to the other body. "That's his brother, Troy."

Hakim glanced up at Major Omar. "His brother?"

The Major nodded. "Yes. And two unregistered Glock 17s found in the pool with them. But no ammunition."

Hakim nodded and studied the face, committing it to memory, then ran his eyes down past the man's face to the neck where a jagged cut across the man's throat pointed to the obvious cause of death.

"Was his brother killed in the same way?"

"Yes." Omar cleared his throat. "The medical examiner estimates the time of death at five to six hours ago, but he can't be certain because the body has been in the water."

Hakim stepped back and nodded to the paramedic, who hurried forward and zipped the body bag shut.

"Who owns the property?" he asked.

"It's registered to a company in Cyprus. We're still tracking down the company owners. But the neighbours say no-one has been here for six months."

Hakim nodded, his eyes drifting over the weeds sprouting from cracks in the pavement and the dead patch of lawn. He turned to look at the property on his right—the still smoldering remains of the Mulroney compound. He knew Liam Mulroney well. In fact, Mulroney paid him a generous sum every month to make sure nothing went wrong with his shipments.

Liam Mulroney differed from others in his line of work. He distributed none of his product in Dubai and, to the outside world, appeared to be a legitimate businessman trading in foodstuffs across North Africa and the Middle East. Colonel Hakim knew otherwise. But he was more than willing to accept the monthly payments and turn a blind eye, as long as Mulroney's illegal dealings stayed offshore.

Hakim had started to question his decisions when Liam requested a roadblock at the entry to The Palm, citing an unspecified threat to his life. Rumors suggested someone was moving in on Liam's business, and judging by the scene in front of him, they might have succeeded. Hakim had been content to look the other way before, but now bodies were turning up on The Palm, questions would inevitably follow.

Colonel Hakim hadn't risen to his rank without a sharp sense of self-preservation, and he wasn't about to risk it now. His phone buzzed again in his pocket. Stepping away from Major Omar and out onto the road, he pulled out the phone —his other phone, the burner he used for off-the-record business. Another call from Liam Mulroney. He had been calling since the early hours, and Hakim's phone screen was filled with missed call notifications. He cursed under his breath and stabbed at the screen with his finger, ending the call.

Hakim slipped the phone back into his pocket and surveyed the scene around him. The paramedics were loading the bodies into waiting ambulances, their lights flashing. Steam rose from the road as water evaporated in the hot sun, while the fire services busied themselves, packing up hoses and equipment, loading them onto the fire trucks.

Omar stood by the entrance gate, speaking into a hand-held radio. He glanced up and raised a hesitant hand toward Hakim. With a sigh, Hakim walked over.

"Sir, they've found some more bodies."

"Where?"

Omar nodded toward Liam Mulroney's villa. "Here, sir."

Hakim shook his head. Whoever it was, it obviously wasn't Liam Mulroney. "Show me."

He followed Omar into the compound, past the fountain in the turning circle, and toward the parking garage. Noticing the bent and twisted garage door, which looked as though it had been struck from the inside, he walked down the ramp. At the bottom, he stopped short—dirty black water, inches deep, covered the garage floor. In front of him, a soot-covered vintage Aston Martin sat alongside a silver Maybach, both vehicles in similar grim condition.

"In the back there, sir."

Behind the cars, a group of policemen and several firemen stood looking down at something.

Hakim looked down at the water and then at his highly polished black leather shoes. He cursed, then stepped forward into the water.

3

The G-Wagen growled slowly through a patch of soft sand, Barry making constant adjustments on the steering wheel, easing on and off the throttle as the SUV's sophisticated four-wheel-drive system hunted for traction.

They had turned off the E44 before reaching the Hatta border crossing, following a track that led into the desert. Despite keeping a go-bag in his office, neither he nor Barry had time to grab it before fleeing the villa, and crossing the border officially without documentation would have been problematic. Liam was hesitant to call in any favors; besides, he preferred to keep his destination under wraps until he knew exactly who he was dealing with.

The sun had risen above the horizon, shining directly into the windshield as they drove eastward through the desert toward the border. The track alternated between soft sand and hard-packed, stony ground, winding its way along the *wadis*—dried-out riverbeds running between the rocky ridges of the Hajar Mountain range. The G-Wagen crunched and scraped over the rough terrain but handled it with ease. Liam was thankful for Barry's quick decision to take the G-Wagen. If they had fled in the Maybach or his vintage Aston, they would've been in serious trouble.

The thought of his Aston and the bullets ricocheting off the body during the gunfight the previous night rekindled the anger he was trying to suppress, and he cursed out loud.

Barry glanced sideways, an eyebrow raised, and Liam made a dismissive gesture with his hand.

"How much longer do you think?"

Barry stuck out his bottom lip. "Another hour at this speed before we hit the highway again."

Liam nodded. "How do you know this route?"

"It's my job to know."

Liam nodded again, satisfied enough with the answer. He relied heavily on Barry for his personal safety, and it wasn't misplaced. They had been together since the beginning and he couldn't think of a more loyal companion.

"Thanks, Barry."

"For what?"

"For saving my life back there."

Barry shrugged but said nothing.

Liam turned his attention back to the landscape. The colors shifted with every mile, from golden sand to rusty red, then grey rock and stone, and back again. Occasionally, splashes of green appeared along the *wadis*, with the odd date palm or acacia offering the only signs of life in the wilderness. It was hard to believe that just a few hours' drive away lay one of the most modern cities in the world. He clenched his teeth. Could he ever return? He had made Dubai his home and loved the city, but until he discovered who had raided his villa, going back would be too risky—especially with the bodies of his men still lying in the compound.

Luckily, Liam was a man who planned for every contingency. It also helped when your business empire generated substantial cash flow.

He maintained a property in Muscat, one he rarely visited but always kept stocked and ready—just in case. That was where they were headed now.

———

4

Approximately three hours after leaving the desert and rejoining the highway, the G-Wagen rumbled steadily through the outskirts of Muscat. Barry kept just under the speed limit, wary of the cameras that monitored speeding and traffic discipline. The less attention they drew, the better.

Liam stifled a yawn. The adrenaline from the past few hours had long since faded, and now the steady hum of the tires on the smooth highway was lulling him into a state of relaxation. He shook his head, trying to stay alert, and glanced over at Barry. His loyal companion hadn't spoken for a while, and dark Ray-Bans hid his eyes, but the lines on his face and the tight set of his jaw made it clear he was just as exhausted.

Just past the Muscat Hills, Barry took the airport exit and entered the suburb of Azaiba, slowing down to maintain a safe distance from the car ahead. Traffic had picked up as people headed to their offices and parents dropped their children at school, though it was nothing compared to rush hour in Dubai. Still, it was heavy enough to keep their pace slow and steady.

About ten minutes later, Barry slowed the car and pulled up in front of a black steel gate set into an immaculate wall that stretched along half the block and around the corner. The wall was too high to offer any glimpse of what lay beyond. The wide footpath outside was spotless, with no litter or sand drifts in sight. At regular intervals, large terra-cotta pots overflowed with vibrant red bougainvillea, adding a touch of beauty. But the plants served a more practical purpose as well—they prevented vehicles and street vendors from occupying the footpath.

Barry gave a toot of the horn and waited. Liam had phoned ahead, so they were expected.

A minute later, the gate slid open, revealing a glimpse of lush green lawns, palm trees, and vibrant flowerbeds—a stark contrast to the dry, sandy streets outside. As they rolled inside and the gate closed behind them, Liam's eyes swept over the single-story white bungalow at the center of the property. It was immaculate, gleaming in the sunlight. To the right stood a more functional-looking two-story building, also whitewashed, which housed his staff. Lined up outside were the staff members: Abdullah, the gardener, his face deeply lined by the harsh desert sun; Joy, the Filipina cook; and Grace, the housemaid from Kenya.

Barry pulled to a stop and Liam unclipped his seatbelt and opened the door, the rush of heat from outside a sudden shock in complete contrast to the pleasantly chilled interior of the G-Wagen. He stood, stretched his back, shook out his legs, then turned and smiled at the staff. They bobbed and curtsied a greeting.

Mahmoud, the watchman, appeared by his side after closing the gate.

"*Marhaban*, sir."

"*Marhaban*, Mahmoud," Liam replied and clasped his shoulder with a welcoming hand. "It's been a while."

"Yes sir, too long sir." Mahmoud looked from him to Barry and then at the vehicle. "Any luggage, sir?"

"Not today, Mahmoud."

Mahmoud looked puzzled but didn't comment. Instead, he gestured toward the house. "Joy has laid out a brunch beside the pool."

"Good." Liam turned and walked toward the bungalow. Joy hurried ahead, with Grace close behind. Liam made his way around the house to the back, where a table was set up in the shade of an old olive tree. At the center of the table was an aluminum tub filled with ice, holding jugs of fruit juice and yogurt. A platter overflowed with fresh fruit, and a basket was filled with warm, freshly baked bread.

Liam nodded approval, pulled out the nearest chair, and sat down. Barry sat on the opposite side of the table with his back to the swimming pool and stretched out his legs.

"Welcome back, sir," Joy greeted him with a smile. "What can I get you?"

"Hello Joy. Bacon and eggs for me." He raised an eyebrow at Barry.

Barry nodded. "Same for me please Joy, and coffee."

Joy nodded and disappeared into the house as Liam reached for the jug of orange juice and poured himself a glass. He held it out to Barry, but Barry shook his head.

Liam took a long sip of the ice-cold juice and sighed. He glanced at Barry and shook his head, the look on his face asking, What the hell happened?

Barry caught the unspoken message, removed his Ray-Bans, tossed them onto the table, and leaned back in his chair. He rubbed his face and stretched his neck from side to side.

Liam studied him closely. The whites of Barry's eyes were bloodshot, and dark smudges shadowed the space beneath them.

"Get some food in ya, Barry, and then grab a couple of hours' kip. There's nothing we can do right now."

Barry let out a deep sigh, his shoulders visibly slumping as if he was finally allowing himself to relax. He leaned forward, grabbed a banana from the fruit platter, and began peeling it. But halfway through, he paused, shaking his head as if lost in an internal debate, then tossed the banana back onto the table.

Looking up at Liam, determination cut through the weariness on his face. "We'll get them, Liam. We'll get them. And when we do, they'll wish they'd never been born."

Liam nodded slowly, his eyes never leaving Barry. He agreed—no one was going to take over his empire.

"One minute," the voice in his earpiece said, and Max took a deep breath, trying to slow his racing heart. It didn't work, but he had expected that.

The familiar surge of adrenaline and cortisol flooded his body. Out of habit, he popped the magazine from his Tavor X95, checked it, then slotted it back in place. His fingers moved over his load vest, confirming everything was in its proper spot, then he took another deep breath. These automatic checks were unnecessary—everything had been checked multiple times—but it kept his mind busy and made the waiting easier. As he glanced around the dimly lit interior of the armored Humvee, he saw his team members doing the same.

His *Samal*, Georges, caught his eye and his teeth flashed white as he grinned. Max nodded a reply and his fingers tightened around his weapon as the voice in his ear said, "Now."

Ariel, the closest to the door, pushed down on the handle and the five men followed him out, each taking up a defensive position to the side of the vehicle, fanning out on the road.

Max glanced up at the sky. Somewhere above them a drone equipped with night vision hovered, giving them valuable over watch, but there was no guarantee they were safe.

At three am the usually bustling streets of Ramallah were quiet, the walls of the buildings glowing amber in the streetlights. A movement ahead caught his eye and instinctively he aimed his weapon, his breath catching in his throat, but then relaxed as a stray cat darted across the road and into the shadows.

The mission was simple: a snatch and grab. The target, Ismail Jabari, was an unemployed teenager who had been on their radar for a while. Always at the forefront of the gangs of stone-throwing youths, he was a known troublemaker. Their orders were to pick him up and bring him in for questioning. Max knew the real objective was to rough him up and scare him, to deter him from future protests and actions. Whether it actually worked, Max couldn't say, but he followed the orders he was given.

Out in front, Georges rose from his crouch and waved them forward. The six men fell into a familiar pattern, three on each side of the street, eyes and weapons constantly scanning the buildings, the doorways, the windows, looking for any danger. They weren't welcome here, and even though it was three am, the threat was real.

The team had rehearsed the mission countless times, poring over maps, satellite images, and even street photos taken by an advance team of undercover operatives. As a result, the streets felt familiar, even in the dark.

The target was two streets away; they had parked the

extraction vehicle out of earshot to make their silent approach on foot.

Moving steadily and quietly, they remained alert, but there was a quiet confidence among them—almost a sense of superiority. They had done this many times before.

Five minutes later, Georges held up his hand, and the men paused. Ahead and to their right was the target's home. A narrow three-story concrete building with a small balcony on each floor overlooking the street. Clothing hung on a drying rack on the lowest balcony and a battered, dust covered Toyota taxi stood at the curb. Ismail's father was the only breadwinner in a town where opportunities for work were few.

Moshe moved forward, a sledgehammer in his hand, and the other men formed up beside him. Max crouched to his right, facing back down the street, his eyes constantly on the move.

"All clear," said the voice in his earpiece. "Go, go, go."

As one, the team stood, switched on the Surefire tactical lights on their weapons and turning their focus on the front door as Moshe stepped forward and with a swing of the sledgehammer hit the door just below the lock. There was a crash and the splintering of wood and the six men rushed forward, filing through the doorway.

Two men cleared the ground floor, an open plan living room and kitchen, while Georges led the way up the stairway past the first floor and up to the top, followed by Ariel, while Max and Moshe took the first floor.

In the background, like a separate soundtrack, Max could hear the shouts of his team and the terrified screams of women. But his focus was on covering Moshe as he drove his boot squarely into the door in front of him. The frame splintered, and the cheaply made door swung inward, hanging from a single hinge. Max's flashlight illuminated the faces of an older couple—the woman scrambling against the wall behind the bed, and the man, hair disheveled and belly protruding from a dirty white vest, shouting back at them.

Max moved past Moshe to the next room and repeated the process, kicking the door with full force and stepping into a dimly lit bedroom. Glow-in-the-dark stars dotted the ceiling, and a nightlight with Ariel, the mermaid, cast a soft glow over the room. Two young girls, Ismail's sisters—one just entering her teens, the other no more than five— screamed in terror, huddling together in the bed they shared.

Max stared down the barrel of his Tavor, his finger resting on the trigger, while the beam of his flashlight caught the glistening tears streaming down the terrified girls' faces.

A voice crackled in his earpiece, "We've got him. Destroy the building."

Without hesitation, Max stepped forward, grabbed the girls with his gloved hand, and yanked them, screaming, from the bed.

6

M ax blinked his eyes open. The room was pitch dark and silent. His heart pounded in his chest, and a shiver ran through him.

The image of the young girls lingered in his mind—their faces streaked with tears, the younger one's lip trembling as she clung to her older sister for protection. A wave of guilt washed over him. He could still feel the weight of his hand pulling them from the bed, their cries echoing in his mind.

He blinked again, shaking off the memory, realizing it was just that—a memory. But it took him a few seconds to remember where he actually was.

Sitting up in bed and looking around, he could just make out the dim shapes of the furniture in the hotel room. He kicked his legs free of the tangled sheets, swung his legs off the bed and peeled the sweat-soaked shirt from his back and chest. Placing his hands on either side of him, he leaned forward, taking a deep breath, at the same time noticing that the sheet beneath him was also soaked with sweat.

He took another long deep breath, holding it for several

beats, then exhaled slowly, the action slowing down his racing heart.

It had been a while since he'd had one of his nightmares. He thought he'd put them behind him, but the stress of the previous night had stirred up the long buried memories.

Sighing, he stood, pulled the shirt over his head, balled it up and tossed it onto the armchair he could just make out in the corner. He did not know what time it was, the blackout curtains doing an excellent job of keeping the daylight out. He padded softly over the carpet towards the windows and pulled the curtains back, blinking violently at the sudden onslaught of blinding sunlight. As his eyes adjusted, he rolled his shoulders back and shook out his arms, feeling the stiffness that had crept into his muscles while he slept. His traps and lats ached, and he raised his right arm above his head and stretched it over to the side before doing the same with his left. He scanned his body for any other aches and pains, but apart from a tightness in his calves, he was okay. Placing his palm on the glass, he felt the heat coming through from the blazing desert sun and as his eyes adjusted to the light, gazed across the body of water he had swum across just a short time ago.

A faint tendril of smoke and steam still rose from the charred remains of the villas at the Mulroney compound. Max reached for the binoculars on the coffee table and raised them to his eyes, focusing on the scene. Where windows once stood were now gaping black holes, with the concrete and stone facade streaked with soot. The palms that had lined the boundary were now reduced to scorched trunks, the fronds that once provided a small amount of shade completely gone.

Several figures in black roamed the grounds, their fire-resistant jackets with high-vis stripes catching the sun. Policemen in their distinctive olive green uniforms accompanied them, and in the lagoon just off the beach, a red Fire Service RIB floated nearby.

Max scanned the neighboring properties and felt a wave of relief. The fire had been contained within the compound, sparing the innocent neighbors. He hadn't considered the possibility of collateral damage when he set the blaze—his only focus had been to destroy any evidence of his presence, but now, he was thankful the fire hadn't spread beyond Mulroney's compound.

There was movement in the compound to the right, and as Max refocused the binoculars, he saw two paramedics pulling one of the guards he had killed from the swimming pool, while a group of policemen looked on.

Max shrugged. He figured the incident would dominate the news for a few days—Dubai wasn't known for shootouts and mass murders—but he was certain something else would soon take its place in the news cycle. He was confident nothing could be traced back to him. The weapon he'd used had come from the Mulroney's, and no one in the city knew who he was.

He set the binoculars on the windowsill and turned away from the view, his growling stomach reminding him he hadn't eaten since the day before. Walking over to the bedside, he picked up the phone and ordered eggs, sausages, and plenty of coffee—enough for two hungry men.

Azar was asleep in the next room, and Max was certain he'd be just as hungry as he was.

As he set the phone down, his thoughts drifted back to his nightmare. That mission had been just one of many he'd carried out during his time in the Israel Defense Force, the

IDF. Back then, he had never questioned his actions. He was trained to follow orders, to do his part in protecting his country from what he believed was an existential threat. But now, those memories didn't sit right with him. The threat had, in many ways, been manufactured by those in power to keep themselves in control. The longer Max served, the more he felt that he and his comrades—men who risked their lives daily—were being used.

A surge of acidity rose in his throat, partly from hunger but also from the old, deeply buried stress and guilt he had carried for so long. He closed his eyes, took a long, deep breath, and exhaled slowly. He hoped, if there was a God— and he had his doubts—that what he had done last night, the lives he had taken, especially Caim Mulroney's, would somehow help to balance the scales. The evil he had fought, even in his small way, might atone for the wrongs of his past. On judgment day, if that was real, he hoped the good he was now doing would count in his favor.

He had rescued Nicola and Tracy and had stopped Caim Mulroney from exploiting young women as mules ever again. But he knew it wasn't enough. There was still much more to do. And he would begin by hunting down Caim's brother, Liam.

7

J ust over five hundred kilometers away, another man woke with a start. His heart pounded in his chest, and his shirt clung to his body, soaked with sweat. But he knew exactly where he was, and as the memories came rushing back, the rage surged within him. Swinging his feet off the bed, he sat up, instantly regretting it as the blast of cold air from the air conditioning hit his damp clothes, chilling him to the bone. He grabbed the remote, switched off the air conditioning, and tossed the remote onto the bed.

A beam of sunlight peeked through a gap in the curtains, cutting across the room, dust motes swirling in the golden light. He peeled the wet shirt from his body, pulling it over his head and dropping it onto the bed. The sheet beneath him was soaked, and the duvet lay in a tangled heap beside him. Taking several deep breaths, he tried to slow his heart rate and quell the anger threatening to overwhelm him, but it barely helped.

Closing his eyes, he rubbed his face, then ran his fingers through his hair before clenching his fists and pounding the mattress in frustration. It had been a long time since he'd felt this way. He had always been in control, always one step ahead. But now, everything felt like it was spiraling out of control. The echoes of gunshots in his underground garage still haunted him, the smell of propellant and hot gun oil lingered in his mind... and the bodies of his men, lying in pools of blood.

"Fuuuuuuck!" he roared, pounding the mattress again in fury.

Taking a deep breath, he straightened up, holding it for a long moment before slowly exhaling. He would fix this, just like he had everything else before. He hadn't clawed his way up from an underprivileged background on the streets of Dublin, only to let it all be taken away by some upstart. He would find out who was behind this, hunt them down to the ends of the earth, and destroy them, their family, and anyone who had helped them. Afterwards, the entire world would think twice before crossing Liam Mulroney. It was time to send a message, to instil fear in the hearts of his competitors.

Feeling more in control, he stood up and walked across the room to the shower, stripping off his clothes before stepping under the hot water. He let it pour over him, relaxing his muscles and washing away the stress. Then, with a sharp twist, he turned the water to cold and forced himself to stand still as the icy blast hit him. After a minute, he shut it off, stepped out, and toweled himself dry. His skin glowed with vitality, and he felt much better—ready to face the day.

Walking into the wardrobe, the light flickered on automatically, sensing his movement. He scanned the row of shirts and selected a plain white linen shirt and loose cream linen pants, laying them on the bed. Then he returned to the ensuite bathroom and stared at himself in the mirror. It almost felt like a stranger looking back—an older version of himself. His face was lined with tension, dark smudges under his eyes, and salt-and-pepper stubble along his jaw.

He shaved the stubble, combed his hair back, and splashed on a generous amount of cologne. Staring straight into his reflection, he thrust his jaw forward. "I'm in control," he told himself. "I'm in control. I'm the king of the jungle. Me, Liam Mulroney. I'm the apex predator, and people fear me." He snarled at his reflection, then slammed his hand down on the vanity, as if punctuating his last statement. Rolling his shoulders back, he walked out into the bedroom to get dressed.

Time to make some calls.

8

"This is it?"

Azar grinned. "Just wait."

Max glanced out the side window of the taxi at the nondescript four-story commercial building on a dusty street in Bur Dubai. There were no signs or markings to indicate what went on inside, and the loading bay door was shuttered and padlocked. It looked as though the bay hadn't been used in months, with piles of garbage and sand collected in the corners. The only sign of activity was the blinking red light on the security camera positioned above the door next to the loading dock.

Max turned his wrist and checked the time on his G-Shock. "Will he be there?"

Azar nodded. "I don't think he ever leaves."

Max frowned and glanced at his friend. "And he's your cousin?"

Azar looked a little sheepish. "Well, not really."

Max shook his head in feigned exasperation. "But you think he can help me?"

"He's the best in the business."

Max looked back at the building and shrugged. Azar hadn't let him down yet, and honestly, Max didn't have any other options.

He reached up, flipped down the sun visor, and checked his reflection in the mirror. Despite managing a few hours of sleep, he still looked exhausted, dark circles under his eyes betraying the strain of the night's events. But outwardly, that was the only trace left of the past twenty-four hours, during which he had killed seven men and set fire to the Mulroney compound. He felt no remorse for the lives he had taken— they had deserved it. He'd long since learned to detach himself from the act of killing. It was the only way to stay sane, compartmentalizing that brutal side of himself and locking it away, only unleashing it when the situation demanded it.

His only regret was that Liam Mulroney had escaped. But with any luck, Azar's contact in the building next to them would help change that.

"Let's go?" he asked.

Azar grunted and opened his door.

Max did the same and stood in the midmorning light, stretching and shaking out the kinks in his legs and back. It had taken them a couple of hours to return from the desert, where he had discarded the weapons used in the raid, reentering Dubai as the morning rush hour clogged the roads. He was grateful now to stand and move, to get the blood flowing around his limbs again. He turned back to the taxi and from the rear seat, removed the CPU he had taken from Liam Mulroney's office and hefted it under his arm before turning back to face the building.

"Lead the way, Azar."

Max followed the Bangladeshi taxi driver up the ramp and stopped beside him as Azar pressed a button on the keypad beside the door and looked up at the blinking camera.

There was a crackle, then a robotic sounding voice, as if Steven Hawking was speaking, sounded from the small speaker on the keypad.

"What do you want?"

Azar cleared his throat, stepped closer, and smiled nervously up at the camera. "Do you remember me? I'm Azar. You helped me with that...." He lowered his voice and looked nervously over his shoulder before continuing, "license issue several months ago."

Max shot a quizzical look at Azar, who shrugged.

"What do you want?" the voice repeated.

Azar gestured at Max. "This is my friend. He needs some help. With a computer."

Max turned slightly, so the CPU under his arm was clearly visible to the camera.

"I don't fix computers," the voice replied.

Max frowned and glanced at Azar, who gave him an encouraging nod.

Max stepped forward and said, "It's not a repair job."

"Then what is it?"

Max glanced back over his shoulder at the street. A white pickup rolled slowly past, but otherwise the street was empty. Turning back to the door, he said, "I would rather discuss this inside."

There was a lengthy pause, then, "I don't know you."

Max sighed loudly and glanced at Azar, jerking his head toward the taxi, suggesting they should leave. But Azar placed a hand on his arm and leaned closer to the keypad. "I can vouch for him. He's a good man. Let us in, and I'll explain."

They both stepped back, looking up at the camera as

they waited. Max, though irritated by the delay, was curious about who—or what—was behind the door.

After what felt like an eternity, the door clicked open.

Azar grinned at Max and pulled the door wider. "Follow me."

9

Ramesh leaned back in his chair, eyes fixed on the security monitors as the two men entered his building.

He recognized Azaruddin Choudary, the Bangladeshi taxi driver. Ramesh had once helped him renew his taxi license despite the lack of proper documents—a simple task for someone with Ramesh's skills. Azaruddin didn't concern him; he was harmless.

But the other man—he was different. Ramesh had recognized his face, though it wasn't until he ran it through facial recognition that he realized why.

Some time ago, another man—someone Ramesh had helped multiple times, a man he deeply respected—had asked him for information on the man now walking down the corridor. Back then, he had been in Sri Lanka. And now he was supposed to be dead.

So what was he doing here?

With one eye on the security monitors to his left, Ramesh skimmed over the information on the main screen in front of him.

Maximillian Klein, Israeli citizen, formerly of the Israel Defence Force, and more recently bodyguard to the disgraced and now deceased Guru Atman. As far as Ramesh was aware, the man walking toward him had died in the recent fire that claimed the life of the Guru in his ashram in India. But here he was, alive and well and seeking Ramesh's help.

Ramesh leaned forward, captured a screenshot of the man's face, and quickly typed a message before hitting send. Then he sat back, watching the men continue their approach. The corridor from the entrance to what he considered his operations center was long, with several security doors the men would need to pass through before reaching him. Their progress was entirely under his control. Whether or not he received a reply wouldn't completely determine his decision—his curiosity about what this man wanted was strong—but a reassuring response would certainly help.

The two men stopped in front of another door and waited, glancing up at the camera. Ramesh pursed his lips, his finger hovering over the button that would release the door. Should he or shouldn't he?

As if in answer, a chime sounded from his monitor. He turned to look at the screen.

Interesting. I would like to know more when you get a chance. You can trust him, but as always, be careful.

Ramesh grinned and tapped the button.

Barry was already outside, pacing by the swimming pool. He glanced up as Liam stepped out, raised a hand in greeting, then returned to his call.

Liam approached the table, which had been cleared of their breakfast, leaving behind only an overflowing ashtray, a silver samovar, and a coffee cup. Glancing at Barry, he noticed he was still wearing the same clothes from earlier, clearly having not slept.

Liam pulled out a chair, sat down facing the pool, and watched Barry continue pacing. He couldn't quite make out the words, but Barry's body language made it obvious he wasn't happy.

Joy appeared in the doorway, and upon seeing Liam, quickly hurried over.

"Sir, can I get you anything?"

Liam pushed thoughts of the crisis from his mind and gave her a big smile. "Joy, thank you. I'm sorry I didn't have time to speak to you when I arrived. I was exhausted."

Joy blushed and bobbed in her version of a curtsey. "It's okay, sir. We are just happy to see you. It's been a long time."

"Indeed, it has, Joy. Several months, I think. How is everything? Is there anything you need?"

"Oh no, sir, thank you. Everything is good."

Liam nodded, still smiling. "And your family? All okay? Is your mother better now?"

Joy's mother had a spell in hospital back in the Philippines earlier in the year, causing Joy considerable distress.

"She is well now, thank you, sir. As long as she stays on the medication."

"That's very good to hear, Joy. Family is important. Our mothers go through so much, bringing us into the world and raising us. It's the least we can do to look after them when they need it. "

"Yes, sir."

"If there is anything you need, just ask. Ok?"

"Yes sir. Thank you, sir. And thank you again for the money you sent. The hospital was very expensive."

Liam gave a dismissive wave of his hand. "It's nothing, Joy. I'm glad she's okay. That's what's important."

Joy nodded, her hands clasped together in front of her. She hesitated, then her eyes went to the table. "Can I get you some more coffee, something to eat?"

"Yes. Fresh coffee, please, lots of it. Thank you."

"Yes, sir." Joy bobbed her head and stepped forward to pick up the samovar and dirty coffee cup.

"Oh, Joy…"

"Sir?"

"Can you bring my phone charger from the bedroom? My battery is almost flat."

She nodded and hurried away as Barry ended the call and made his way toward him from the far side of the swimming pool.

"You didn't sleep?"

Barry shook his head, pulled out a chair, and sat down with a sigh.

"You need to rest, Barry. I need you in top form if we're going to get through this."

"I'll sleep later," Barry growled and tossed his phone onto the table.

Liam nodded at the phone. "Any luck?"

Barry made a face and shook his head. "Nothing. I checked with all our informants. No-one knows anything."

"Shit. Who the fuck are these guys?"

"It gets worse."

"How can it get any worse?"

Barry was about to speak when Joy appeared with the phone charger in her hand. "I'll tell you," he said and waited as Liam passed her his phone and told her to plug it into the outdoor socket beside the table.

Once Joy had returned to the house, Barry sat forward in his chair, leaning his forearms on the table, and looked Liam directly in the eyes. "The compound is destroyed. Gutted by fire."

"Fuck!" Liam exclaimed and thumped his fist on the table. "Fuck," he repeated. He looked up as a thought entered his mind. "Caim?"

Barry winced and broke eye contact. He opened his mouth to say something, then closed it again.

"Well, out with it, man!"

Barry looked up, a look of sorrow crossing his face. "Dead."

Liam clenched his fist, his face screwed up in anger, and went to punch the tabletop but just regained control. He shook his fist, ground his teeth, then released his fist and slumped back in his chair.

"Stupid little fucker," he said, shaking his head. "Stupid

stupid little...." He trailed off, staring at the tabletop in front of him.

Barry remained silent, giving Liam time to grieve.

Liam remained silent for a long time, even as Joy brought out the coffee. His brother had always been a pain in the arse, and Liam had bailed him out more times than he could count. But family was family.

Barry poured two cups of coffee, sliding one over to Liam. Liam stared at it for a moment before pulling himself together. Looking up, he asked, "Hakim told you all this?"

Barry shook his head. "He's not taking any calls. Fortunately, I've got another contact—junior, but useful."

Liam nodded, scowling. "It's time I cash in my insurance and remind Hakim where his loyalties should lie."

An electric lock buzzed, and the door in front of them clicked open. Like the three doors they'd already passed through, there was no sign of what lay beyond, just a camera overhead with a blinking light, the only sign that they were being monitored.

Azar glanced over his shoulder, grinned, and pushed through the door.

Max followed, pausing in the doorway to take in his surroundings. They were in a large, dimly lit room filled with the hum of cooling fans and the soft beeping of electronics. To his left, several racks of servers stood, with a tangled web of power cables snaking across the floor, up the walls, and into a duct. On the right was a rudimentary kitchen, complete with a fridge, a small gas cooktop, and a pile of dirty dishes. In stark contrast to the clutter, a gleaming La Marzocco coffee machine sat beside the stack of dishes.

Max registered all of this in an instant, but his attention was fixed on the figure seated at the far end of the room. The man was silhouetted against a bank of monitors, leaning back in an office swivel chair, one leg crossed over the other, elbows resting on the armrests, and fingers steepled in front of his face. He appeared to be of slight build, and from what Max could make out in the dim light, he guessed the man was from the same region as Azar.

"Good morning, Ramesh." Azar seemed a little nervous, his smile forced, and he looked back at Max as if for reassurance.

Max frowned. Who was this person?

The man ignored the greeting and addressed his question to Max. "You said you would explain."

Max shifted the CPU under his arm, adjusting the weight. "Azar said you can help me find out what's on this." He nodded toward the CPU under his arm.

"I'm guessing it doesn't belong to you."

Max shrugged. "Possession is nine-tenths of the law."

The man called Ramesh gave a soft laugh, but said nothing.

"Well, can you?" Max asked.

Ramesh tapped his fingers together rhythmically. "I know nothing about you. How do I know you aren't doing anything illegal?"

Azar glanced back at Max, a look of concern clouding his face.

Max gave a half smile. "I'm guessing, by your setup here, that not everything you do is on the right side of the law."

Ramesh shrugged.

"I'm not doing anything illegal. But, there may be information about illegal activities on this CPU." Max nodded toward Azar, "Azar said you could help me find out what's on here, and he said you would be discreet. I trust Azar. I hope I can trust you."

"What did you say your name was?"

"I didn't."

Ramesh waited.

"Max. You can call me Max."

"Max," Ramesh repeated. "Short for Maximilian?"

Max's heart skipped a beat, but he avoided any change of expression. "No, just Max. So, can you help me or not?"

"Well, just Max, whatever is discussed in this room stays in this room. You do not need to worry about my discretion."

"Ok."

"And there is no computer in the world that I cannot access."

"Good. What will it cost me?"

Ramesh waved a hand. "Let's see what's on this computer first." He swivelled in his chair, reached behind him and tapped a key on his keyboard. Bright light flooded the room, blinding Max momentarily.

Once his eyes had adjusted, he studied the man in front of him. He was young, slightly built, and despite being Indian, his skin was pale, almost a sickly grey, as if he saw little sunlight. He wore a pair of rimless glasses and his hair needed a wash and a cut.

Ramesh grinned at him. "Bring it over here."

Max glanced at Azar, who nodded, then turned back to Ramesh. After a brief hesitation, he stepped forward and placed the CPU on the spot Ramesh had indicated on the bench.

Ramesh got to work, plugging in cables while Max scanned the monitors. One displayed lines of code scrolling rapidly, another flashed with Forex rates, while a bank of screens showed feeds from the security cameras. Off to the side, a muted television displayed a newsfeed.

Once Ramesh finished connecting the cables, he rolled his chair to the side and began typing commands into his keyboard. He glanced up at the monitor in front of him, muttering something under his breath.

"A problem?"

Ramesh shook his head. "No. Not really. It's password protected, but I can deal with that." He entered another command, then sat back in his chair and turned to face Max.

"I have a program that will crack the password. We just need to give it time."

Max nodded, his eyes on the screen, watching the numbers and letters change rapidly as Ramesh's program hunted through the password possibilities.

"How long will it take?" he asked.

"I don't know. Are you in a hurry?"

Max frowned and looked down at the young Indian man. "I don't know."

Ramesh raised an eyebrow. "You don't know?"

"Well, it depends."

Ramesh nodded slowly, "Depends on what's on this?"

Max nodded.

Azar cleared his throat. "Um... I will need to get to work at some stage."

"Why don't you go Azar? This could take some time. I'll look after Max here for you. I can call you when we're done."

Azar looked worried. "Is that okay, Max?"

Max nodded and smiled. "Of course, Azar. I'll call you later."

Azar hesitated for a moment, then nodded. "Okay."

Max turned to Ramesh. "I'll just see him out."

Ramesh nodded and returned his focus to the monitors.

Max walked with Azar back to the door, pulled it open,

and waited for Azar to step through before following him down the corridor.

Azar started to say something, but Max interrupted. "Not here, outside."

They reached the outer door and Max pressed the door release. It clicked open, and they both stepped outside into the sunlight. Max took Azar by the arm and led him away from the doorway. Turning his back on the camera, he asked in a low voice, "Are you sure he can be trusted?"

Azar nodded. "Yes. I'm sure."

"How did you find out about him?" Max asked, realising he should probably have asked this question before handing over the CPU.

"A friend needed a passport... a false one. Ramesh arranged it for him. And then I got him to renew my taxi license." Azar gave a guilty grin. "I don't have any documents, but it wasn't a problem for Ramesh." He put a hand on Max's arm. "He's good Max. He can do anything with computers."

Max pursed his lips, watching Azar's face. He didn't really have any other option and besides, Ramesh didn't know who he was. He figured he was safe.

"Okay," he nodded. "I'll see what he can do. I'll call you later." He slapped Azar on the shoulder. "Thank you, my friend."

He waited while Azar walked out toward his taxi and climbed in, then turned back to the entrance, pressed the entry buzzer, and looked up at the camera.

12

W hen Max was buzzed back into the room, Ramesh was sitting facing the door, arms crossed and head tilted to one side.

Max stopped in the middle of the room, waiting for Ramesh to speak. It was clear something was weighing on his mind.

"I know who you are."

Max's heart skipped a beat, but kept his expression neutral. "What do you mean?"

Ramesh smiled with one side of his face. "I mean, I know who you really are."

Max took a breath and frowned. "I still don't understand what you're trying to say."

Ramesh grinned. "Maximilian Klein, former Israel Defence Force. But more recently, bodyguard to the disgraced Guru Atman who died in his ashram just a couple of days ago."

Max could feel the blood drain from his face, but again, he fought to maintain his composure. How the hell did this man know all this?

"Your secret is safe with me, Max," Ramesh continued. "I've been told I can trust you, and I want to let you know you can trust me."

"Okay," Max replied, determined to be as non-committal as possible. "You trust Azar's judgement so much?"

Ramesh chuckled. He swivelled in his chair and turned his attention back to the monitor. "Not so much Azar," he looked back over his shoulder, "more like John Hayes."

Max stood stunned, not sure what to say. He stared at the young Indian man as he typed away on his keyboard, glancing from monitor to monitor as if the conversation hadn't happened.

He cleared his throat. "How do you know John Hayes?"

"It's a long story," Ramesh muttered, his attention fixed on the monitor. He paused in his typing and spoke as if he was addressing the monitor in front of him. "Aren't you supposed to be dead?"

Max shrugged, still puzzled as to how things were playing out. "Also a long story."

Ramesh waved toward the coffee machine. "Help yourself to some coffee. You look tired..... dead tired," he chuckled at his joke. "You can make me one too while you're at it. We have a lot to talk about."

Max hesitated, still frowning, then shrugged and walked over to the machine.

"Do you know how to use it?"

"I'll work it out."

"Black, three sugars."

Max studied the machine, working out where everything was. To the side was a grinder and a black airtight container. He removed the top and looked inside, finding the beans. Removing the container from the top of the grinder, he set it on a small scale on the bench top and zeroed it.

"Twenty grams," Ramesh called out from his workstation as if he had eyes in the back of his head. "I want a double shot."

"I know," Max grunted. He had used a very similar machine before, back when he was a bodyguard. Atman, the guru he had been protecting, never skimped on luxuries, despite constantly preaching a simple life to his followers. His private quarters in all his ashrams were equipped with top-of-the-line coffee and kitchen equipment, staffed by trained chefs—all funded by his loyal followers or skimmed from the money he laundered for politicians and businessmen.

Max focused on grinding the beans, transferring the ground coffee to the portafilter as he used the moment to think about his current situation. He had discarded all traces of his previous life off the coast of India. His British passport was genuine but carried a fake name: Max Jones. As far as he knew, no one in Dubai had any idea who he was —until now.

He looked around for the sugar while the hot water trickled through the coffee grounds. Should he just cut his losses and get out of there? But then a vision of the G-Wagen escaping up the road while he stood in the driveway of Liam Mulroney's compound flashed before his eyes. If he left now, his chances of finding Liam were almost non-existent. But if he stayed and found out what was on the CPU, then maybe he had a chance.

He found a container with a brown powder and held it close to his face, sniffing it. Jaggery. He recognized it—unrefined, powdered cane sugar from India. "You want the jaggery or sugar?"

"Jaggery. White sugar will kill you," came the reply.

Max shook his head. "Jaggery is still sugar."

Ramesh didn't respond, the only sound the frantic tapping of keys on the keyboard.

Max stirred the jaggery into Ramesh's coffee, repeated the process without sugar for his own coffee, and carried it over. He set it down beside Ramesh and then stood, his coffee cup in his hand, and looked at the lines of code scrolling across the screen.

Ramesh jerked his head towards a chair to his right. "Grab a seat."

Max pulled the wheeled chair closer, sat down, and took a sip of his espresso. It was strong, with notes of chocolate. He had been on the go since two that morning, having only eaten two protein bars and drunk a bottle of water, and his energy levels were running low. Fatigue was settling into his bones, and his stomach growled as the rich coffee slid down his throat.

"So why don't you tell me how a dead man is sitting next to me sipping coffee?" Ramesh asked.

Max stared into his coffee cup, contemplating for a moment before replying, "You have me at a considerable disadvantage. It seems you know a lot more about me than I do about you."

Ramesh paused in his typing and gave a small nod.

Max continued, "So perhaps you first tell me how you know so much and what your connection is with John Hayes?"

Ramesh typed another command, then hit the enter key with a flourish. He turned in his seat, reached for his coffee cup, and faced Max. He seemed to be assessing him. Sipping his coffee, he then licked his lips, nodding with satisfaction.

"Okay." He smiled. "Why not? John says I can trust you and I have a lot of time for John. Besides...." he flicked his eyes toward the screen, "this is going to take a while."

13

By the time Ramesh had finished explaining how he knew John Hayes, Max had decided to trust him. There were gaps in Ramesh's story, as there naturally would be—he didn't need to share every detail—but it was clear enough that the young Indian man would be on his side.

Max spent the next five minutes summarizing his escape from India under the cover of darkness, fleeing to Dubai with a false passport, and, without going into too much detail, explained how he had ended up in Ramesh's company.

"So the shootout on The Palm last night was you?"

Max shrugged.

Ramesh grinned. "Knowing your background, I'm not surprised you could pull it off, but Azar surprises me."

"He's been very helpful."

"Hmmm, so it seems." Ramesh fell silent, looking down at his feet while tapping a rhythm on his armrest with his fingertips. After a lengthy pause, he looked up. "Okay. I'm going to help you, just as I've helped John in the past. We all make mistakes in life, take the wrong path, but only a select few recognize their errors and try to make amends. What Atman was doing was disgusting, and it's good that he's gone. That you've realized this and are willing to make amends is commendable."

He paused, glancing around the room, his eyes darting across the bank of monitors. "I skirt the law, Max. I do things that aren't necessarily legal, but my crimes are financial and aimed at those who can afford it—big corporations, governments, for instance. Rarely individuals. I make money in the markets, trade information, and help people like Azar with false documents and that sort of thing. I get a kick out of it. But after meeting John, I've realized that nothing gives me more satisfaction than fighting injustice."

Max nodded.

"So, I'll help you in whatever way I can. And I'll do it for free. Just cover any expenses."

"Thank you, Ramesh."

Ramesh nodded and swivelled in his chair. He pulled the keyboard closer and began typing. "Liam Mulroney, you said?"

Max grunted in agreement and leaned forward in the chair, his eyes fixed on the screen in front of Ramesh. Multiple windows opened faster than he could read them, as Ramesh typed rapidly, entering commands and rearranging the windows on his screen.

"So he runs a trading company... foodstuffs and commodities through Northern Africa and the Middle East..... Irish citizen, long-time resident in Dubai. Property on the Palm," Ramesh paused and glanced at Max, before continuing, "other properties in Dubai, residential, commercial,....several bank accounts..... director of....woah.... many companies.... So on the face of it, a successful European businessman."

"How can you read all that so quickly?"

Ramesh shrugged. "Practise. I've been doing it since I was a kid." He turned to look at Max. "We all have our skills. I'm sure you can do many things I would never dream of doing."

Max simply nodded, non-committal. He could never spend his days holed up in a windowless room, staring at a screen. He needed sunlight—the brighter, the better—movement, and the feel of the wind on his skin. He doubted Ramesh got outside much, but he had to admit the young man seemed incredibly skilled with computers.

At that moment, one of the monitors beeped, and Ramesh glanced at the screen. A smile spread across his face, and he chuckled. "See, I told you I could get in." He turned to grin at Max. "Now let's see what you've brought me."

14

Colonel Hakim Al-Hamadi slammed the phone down and rubbed his head in frustration. The day had gone from bad to worse. That was the tenth call he'd received since returning to the office, and they were all about the same thing: the massacre on The Palm.

By the time he left the smoldering ruins of the Mulroney compound, seven bodies had been discovered. Even with the burns, it was clear that some had been shot. One of those was suspected to be Liam Mulroney's brother, Caim. It wasn't confirmed yet, but the remains of a body had been found on the top floor of Caim Mulroney's villa, with a bullet hole in the skull.

Nothing like this had ever happened in Dubai before. Fires, yes, but a mass shooting? Never. Hakim exhaled loudly and shook his head. Many criminals called Dubai home, but for most, their crimes occurred elsewhere. Dubai was safe—a haven for both lawbreakers and law-abiding citizens, a place where criminals sanitized their images and erased their pasts. An incident like this was the last thing Hakim needed in a career that had so far been unblemished. The pressure from his superiors to uncover the truth was immense.

This situation would demand all the cunning and strategic intelligence of a man who had navigated the system while treading the line between legal and illegal activities. He had never committed a crime himself, but he accepted money from those who did. He had one guiding principle: do what you want, as long as it wasn't in Dubai. Who was he to judge an expatriate's activities in their own country? As long as it wasn't happening in Dubai, they weren't breaking the law in his eyes. But this was different. This was on his soil. He swivelled in his chair, crossed his bare feet, and stared out the window. His socks and shoes were lined up on the windowsill, drying in the sun. He didn't have time to go home and change, and hoped they dried before the press conference later that day.

The sun blazed down on the car park of the Al Barsha Police Station, but Hakim barely noticed. His mind was filled with thoughts of how to salvage his reputation and deliver a satisfactory outcome for his superiors.

The calls from Liam Mulroney had finally stopped—praise be to Allah—but he knew he couldn't ignore him forever. Eventually, he would need to speak with him.

There was a gentle knock on the door and a hesitant, "Sir?"

He swiveled in his chair to see a constable standing in the doorway. "What is it?"

"This just came for you, sir." The constable held up a manila envelope.

Hakim reached out for it and studied it. It was blank, with just his name typed on the front. No return address. "Did you see who brought this in?"

"No, sir. It was on the front desk when I got back from my break."

"Okay," Hakim shrugged. "Can you get someone to bring me some coffee?"

"Yes, sir."

The constable saluted and hurried away, while Hakim reached for a letter opener from his pen stand and slit the envelope open and looked inside.

There were three large photos, and he pulled them out and stared at the glossy black-and-white image on the first one.

His breath stopped, and his heart rate accelerated.

"Ya kalb!"

15

Hakim was still staring at the envelope when the coffee arrived. He barely acknowledged the constable and then ignored the coffee his system had been craving just a short time earlier.

The photos were back in the envelope, and it now sat in the middle of his desk. He was almost afraid to touch it again.

As if the day hadn't been bad enough already, it was now a disaster of monumental proportions.

Hakim was a family man, like all good Emiratis. He had a loving wife at home and two beautiful daughters, Aaliyah and Sariah, aged six and eight. He loved them deeply and would do anything for them, and he resented the time spent away from his little girls, who believed their father could do no wrong.

But Hakim had needs—needs his wife no longer fulfilled. She was a good woman, but since the birth of their children, Latifah could not satisfy those appetites.

So, Hakim sought release elsewhere. In his mind, he was doing nothing wrong. He wasn't harming anyone, and there was no emotional attachment; it was purely a physical release.

But his family would see it differently. And his superiors? They wouldn't look kindly upon his extracurricular activities, even if many of them probably indulged in similar pursuits.

He ground his teeth together, aware of his racing heart. Reaching for the coffee, he noticed his fingers were visibly trembling and decided against drinking it. It would only make things worse. There was no way he would feel sleepy after what he'd seen in the envelope. Yesterday had started off so well—how quickly things could change in just twenty-four hours.

His phone buzzed in his pocket, and he pulled it out to check the screen. It was the burner phone, and upon seeing the name displayed, he realized who had sent him the envelope. An envelope and photos that could ruin his life if they ever became public.

He stood up, crossed the room, and closed the door behind him before returning to his desk, the phone still buzzing in his hand.

Taking a deep breath, he answered the call.

16

"So you finally decide to take my call," Liam growled into the phone.

"Ya ibn el sharmouta!"

Liam spoke little Arabic, but he knew when he was being cursed.

"Hey, steady on Hakim. I'm not the one who's been sticking my willy into Russian prostitutes, am I? I'm sure your wife wouldn't appreciate finding out what you get up to in your spare time."

Liam heard Hakim curse again and glanced up at Barry, who was listening to the call on speakerphone.

Barry met his gaze, his expression revealing nothing.

On the other end of the line, Liam heard a heavy sigh. "What is that you want?"

"Now, Hakim *habibi*, don't be like that. We were on such good terms before and there's no reason we can't continue in the same way. But I expect you to answer the phone when I call you."

"What did you expect me to do?" Hakim protested. "I've

been at your property all morning, pulling dead bodies out of the neighbour's pool and scraping burnt flesh off the floor of your villa. Do you think I have time to deal with phone calls?" Hakim asked, a hint of anger creeping into his voice.

"Now calm down there wee fella," Liam replied, a thick Irish brogue long since hidden, creeping back into his voice. "The only call I want you to worry about is mine. Otherwise, the next call I make is to your lovely wife...... Latifah, isn't it?"

Hakim cursed again, this time making a more muted sound.

"Will you take my calls?" Liam pushed for an answer.

"*Na'am*....... yes."

"Good. I knew you would see the sense in cooperating. Now tell me, what do you know about last night?"

Liam heard Hakim take a deep breath and exhale loudly.

"Nothing at all. All I know is we have seven dead bodies, a burnt out villa, and eyewitness reports of gunshots."

"And you know one of those bodies belongs to my brother?"

There was a moment of silence, and then when Hakim spoke, the anger was gone. "Yes Liam, I'm sorry."

Liam screwed up his face and clenched his fist, but fought to maintain control.

"All the more reason for you to pick up when I call, Hakim."

Hakim said nothing, just the sound of his breathing heard over the speaker.

Liam leaned forward, his face over the phone on the table. "How did he die? The fire killed him? I bet he was drunk."

Again there was a longer silence than normal then the

sound of Hakim clearing his throat. "Ah, no. He was ah....
executed. Gunshot wound to the head."

Liam screwed his eyes shut, his fingertips turning white
as he dug them into the tabletop. It felt as if a knife had
been plunged into his heart, and tears welled in his eyes. He
tried to speak, but his throat constricted. In the distance, he
could hear Barry's voice asking Hakim if he had any leads.
He couldn't make out Hakim's response, as images of his
brother flashed before him—memories from their youth on
the streets of Dublin and later in Dubai. He recalled his
brother's smile, his laughter, and that ridiculous dance he
did when he was drunk, which had become more frequent
in recent years.

Though everything that had just happened was Caim's
fault, Liam regretted that their last words had been filled
with anger. Taking a deep breath, he opened his eyes,
ignoring the tear that trickled down his right cheek, and
looked up at Barry.

His friend, his right-hand man, his loyal companion,
looked back at him, sorrow mirrored in the big man's eyes.
Liam took another deep breath and sat up straight, curling
his fingers in to a fist.

"I want you to find out who did this, Hakim."

"My men are working on it, but right now there are no
leads. No-one saw anything. It's as if it's the work of a *djinn*."

Liam slammed his fist down on the table, causing the
phone to jump. "It's no motherfuckin' *djinn,* you stupid,
superstitious fuck," He roared down the phone. "There's no
such thing. This is the work of a powerful group who are
trying to take over my business. You do everything you can
to find out who it is and you tell me everything you know.
Because if you don't, I'm taking you down with me.
Understand?"

There was no reply.

"Do you understand?" he demanded again.

"Yes," came the grudging reply.

"Good. I want a report twice a day, and when I call, I expect you to pick up the motherfucking phone!" and Liam stabbed his finger at the screen, ending the call.

17

"So, what exactly are you looking for?" Ramesh asked, scanning the screen.

Max made a face and shook his head. "I... I don't know, to be honest. Just some clues about where Liam Mulroney might be now."

"Hmmm, okay," Ramesh muttered, his fingers flying across the keyboard. Files opened and closed on the screen, moving around faster than Max could keep track of.

"This is going to take some time." Ramesh leaned back in his chair and turned to face Max. "Are you any good with computers?"

Max pouted his lips and shrugged. "No worse than anyone else, I suppose, but I wouldn't be here if I had your skills."

"No." Ramesh nodded, studying Max for a moment. Then he gestured toward another monitor and keyboard. "Sit over there. We'll split this up." He spun back in his chair and resumed tapping on the keyboard. "I'm sending half the files to that monitor. Start looking through them. Maybe it will be quicker."

Max nodded, took a seat where directed, and began opening the files.

Several hours later, the passage of time in the windowless room was only marked by the clock at the top of the screen. Max leaned back in his chair and rubbed his eyes, feeling sick. The lack of sunlight and hours spent staring at the artificial light had drained him of the little energy he had left. He needed to be outside, moving around, breathing fresh air.

He had sifted through hundreds of business reports, documents, and bills of lading, but nothing made much sense to him. All he had gathered was that Liam Mulroney owned multiple companies across various jurisdictions, shipped foodstuffs throughout the Middle East, and had numerous bank accounts. He also owned properties in the Middle East, the UK, and Ireland. He could be at any of them—or none.

Frustrated, he blew air through pursed lips and stretched his neck from side to side. Looking over at Ramesh, he marveled at how the young man continued working, seemingly unaffected by the airless, soulless environment. His eyes darted across multiple screens as his fingers flew over the keyboard, entering commands and managing several tasks at once.

"Found anything?" Max asked.

"Not yet," came the reply. "But it's only a matter of time."

Max didn't share Ramesh's confidence. In fact, he couldn't face spending more time staring at the screen. He pushed back his chair and stood up. "I need some fresh air. I'm going for a walk."

"Okay." Ramesh didn't even look up.

Max pulled out his phone. "Give me your number."

Ramesh recited his phone number, and Max tapped it into his phone and dialled. "I'm giving you a missed call. Call me if you find anything."

"Yup," Ramesh muttered, still typing.

Max shook his head and gave a wry smile. This life was not for him.

He walked out of the room and down the long corridor, passing through a series of doors until he reached the exit. Pressing the door release, he stepped outside. The light was so much brighter than inside that he blinked for a moment until his eyes adjusted, then made his way down onto the street. The sun hit his face and arms, making him feel as if he was being recharged. He turned his face toward the sky, closed his eyes, and took a deep breath. It wasn't fresh air— the smell of exhaust fumes and other chemicals made his nostrils twitch—but it was better than being indoors.

A car honked its horn, snapping him back to reality. He opened his eyes and looked around. A pickup truck rolled past with several laborers sitting in the rear, every inch of their bodies covered to shield them from the harsh desert sun, leaving only their eyes visible. Across the street, a thin cat stretched and yawned before sauntering away. There was no one else around.

He glanced left, then right, unsure of where to go, then shrugged. It didn't really matter, and began walking.

18

H akim hadn't moved for an hour, his coffee cold and untouched on the desk beside him. He ignored the phone calls that came in, and whenever anyone knocked on his door, he yelled, "Go away!"

His gaze remained fixed on the envelope lying on his desk, positioned next to a framed picture of Latifah and their daughters. The contents threatened not only to destroy his career but also everything he held dear. Latifah would never forgive him, but even more troubling was the thought of how his daughters would react.

He felt physically sick, a heavy weight pressing down on his chest, churning his stomach. Why couldn't he keep his urges under control? What was wrong with him? He gritted his teeth in frustration. If he ever got out of this unscathed, he vowed he would never look at another woman again. Reaching for the envelope, he opened the drawer of his desk and slid it inside, then swiveled in his chair to gaze out the window.

A patrol car drove into the parking lot, and he watched as it cruised past the rows of parked vehicles before pulling into an empty spot. The doors opened, and the driver and passenger climbed out—two constables in uniform, laughing and sharing a joke, playfully patting each other on the back.

A part of him longed for the days when he had just graduated from the Dubai Police Academy, when everything was fresh and he had no responsibilities weighing him down.

He sighed and checked his watch. Enough feeling sorry for himself; he needed to find a solution. Right now, that meant discovering who had attacked the Mulroney compound. What Liam Mulroney did with that information was up to him, and Hakim would deal with the fallout when the time came.

He reached for his desk phone and pressed a number.

"Send Major Al-Farsi in as soon as possible."

"Yes, sir."

Leaning back in his chair, with his elbows resting on the armrests, he steepled his fingers in front of his face. The attacker had to be someone moving in on Liam Mulroney's business—another dealer, perhaps.

That's where he would start.

19

M ax had wandered aimlessly for about an hour through the back streets of Bur Dubai until the sun became too intense, and his body craved the coolness of air conditioning. Although he was used to the desert sun, having grown up in Israel and spent many days patrolling in full combat gear on the streets of Gaza and the West Bank, he wasn't one to punish himself unnecessarily. Air conditioning was invented for a reason, and after getting his fill of the outdoors, he considered heading back to Ramesh's bunker.

He pulled out his phone and dialed Ramesh.

"Yes?" came the response.

"Have you found anything?"

"Not yet... well, I've come across some encrypted files, but I haven't accessed them yet."

"Okay." Max gazed up the dusty street, noticing two bearded men in long shirts and baggy cotton pants leaning against a pickup, deep in conversation. A young boy, perhaps in his early teens, unloaded boxes from the truck.

As he observed the scene, he thought about what he would do if he were Liam Mulroney. Where would he go?

The sound of Ramesh typing and muttering to himself came through the phone speaker. "Ramesh, can you send me the list of properties he owns? I'll start by checking them out. There's a boat too, right?"

"Yes. It's in the Port Saeed Marina."

"Good. I'll look into that. In the meantime, let me know if you find anything."

"Will do." The line went dead without a goodbye, and Max grinned. At least Ramesh was focused.

His phone buzzed almost immediately with a message, and he glanced at the screen. Ramesh had sent him the information he requested. Max tapped on the screen to open the PDF. It contained a list of properties sorted by location—around ten in Dubai. He would start with those, but first, he needed transportation.

He called Azar.

20

S everal hours later, Max was only a third of the way through the list.

Azar had picked him up within half an hour of his call, his face beaming with happiness and eagerness to help Max again. Max offered a generous fee to hire his taxi for the day, though deep down, he suspected Azar would have done it for free. The friendly Bangladeshi man was excited about what he called "undercover" work.

Max grinned as he climbed back into the taxi. Using Azar made sense; taxis were so common on the streets of Dubai that they were almost invisible. No one would suspect a taxi passenger of conducting surveillance, and it helped that Azar knew the city intimately. Plus, it was good to have company. Azar kept him entertained between properties with stories about his childhood growing up on the streets of Dhaka and how he had heard of great fortunes being made by his fellow countrymen in Dubai. He had worked for five years before saving enough money to pay an agent who promised him a high-paying job upon his arrival in the city, but it all turned out to be a scam. There was no job, and he never heard from the agent again.

"No luck?" Azar turned in his seat, looking at Max with concern.

Max shook his head and glanced out the window at the warehouse he had just inspected. "Empty." Frustration crept in, but he shook it off. So far, he had visited three properties, all warehouses—two empty and one in use—but there had been no sign of Liam. He reasoned with himself that there were still more properties to check. If Liam was hiding out, why would he choose a warehouse? Max suspected he was on his boat, and he was saving that for last. "What's next, Azar?"

Azar studied the list of addresses Max had shared and looked up. "A villa in Green Community Village. About twenty minutes from here."

"Okay, let's go."

Azar put the car in gear and pulled away from the curb. "So, I did a lot of odd jobs," he continued from where he had left off before Max got out of the car. "I worked in a warehouse just like this one, and in restaurants. All for cash. The work was hard, and the pay terrible, but..." He looked up into the mirror, his eyes meeting Max's. "I couldn't go home. The agent kept my passport, and my wife and family depended on me."

"Yeah," Max nodded, exhaling loudly in sympathy. "So, how did you end up driving a taxi?"

Azar checked his wing mirror before signaling and changing lanes.

"It took me two years, Max. Working nonstop, sending everything I earned back home. I lived in one room, sharing it with three other men. Sometimes I only had one meal a day." He looked up into the mirror, his eyes twinkling. "I was very thin, not like now."

Max grinned back. Azar certainly didn't look like he skipped meals now.

"Then I met Ramesh." Again, Azar looked up into the mirror, catching Max's attention. "He's a good man, Max. He's helped many people like me. He helped me get a new passport and arranged the documents I needed for a taxi license." Azar turned to look back over his shoulder, a big grin on his face. "Now I have my own flat. You should come visit sometime."

Max nodded toward the road ahead. "I will, but if you don't keep your eyes on the road, neither of us will see the end of today."

Azar bobbed his head and grinned, then turned back to face the front.

Max stared out the window at the buildings flashing by. The world was a fascinating place. Once barren desert sand had transformed into one of the richest cities in the world, attracting business people from all corners of the globe. The wealth in this city of four million people was unfathomable. Yet, beneath the glitz and glamour lay a dark underside where people like Azar were exploited and cheated, their passports taken and made to work like slaves on construction sites and in factories. Then there was the blind eye turned toward the source of that wealth—funds siphoned from government contracts, stolen from companies, or the proceeds of crime—drugs, guns, prostitution—while the perpetrators lived outwardly respectable lives in the Emirates.

Max turned to look at Azar, a hardworking man living away from home, toiling long hours so his family could have a chance at a better life. His daughter would graduate, the first in their family to receive a college education, and she would likely go on to achieve great things—all because of the sacrifices her father had made. In stark contrast, there was Liam Mulroney, living in comfort, amassing great wealth, all at the expense of others' suffering. By capitalizing on addiction and supplying a product that ruined lives. Max grimaced. Life wasn't fair.

He recalled his nightmare, the terrified girls he had dragged from their beds in the dead of night before demolishing their home—all because their brother had thrown stones at soldiers who shouldn't have been there in the first place. A wave of guilt washed over him, and he allowed it to grow until it filled him, then transformed it into anger and determination. He could never solve the world's problems, but he would do his best to do good. He would strive to make his corner of the world, his field of influence, a better place. A simple man like Azar, driving a taxi and living a modest life so his family could benefit, was a better person than Max had been, and Max planned to use him as an example of how to become a better man himself.

A n idea had been forming in the back of Max's mind throughout the day, and as Azar turned off Sheikh Rashid Road into Port Saeed Marina, it began to take shape.

As the taxi rolled slowly in, they passed a small tavern on the right, with empty outside tables baking in the afternoon sun. Then, at the T-junction, Azar slowed to a stop and glanced into the mirror for instructions. Max leaned forward between the seats, peering through the windshield. The left fork led toward the outer part of the marina, where super-yachts were moored. He had researched Liam Mulroney's boat—a twenty-one meter Azimuth 66, large enough to accommodate up to ten people. In Dubai, however, that was considered small, and its mooring was likely with the other "small" boats.

"Take the right."

Azar nodded and turned right while Max gazed at the boats moored to their left.

"Park here on the left," he instructed, pointing to some empty parking spaces near a row of restaurants.

Azar parked the taxi and looked back over his shoulder with a questioning eyebrow.

"Are you hungry?" Max asked.

Azar grinned. "Always."

"Good." Max turned to look out the back window. "There's a Thai restaurant. Grab us a table and order some food while I go for a walk."

Azar turned to eye the restaurant, doubt crossing his face. He looked down at his clothes, then back at Max. "It looks fancy," he mumbled.

Max reached forward and gripped Azar's shoulder. "Be confident, my friend. Just walk in and ask for a table for two outside. They won't say no. You're a customer."

Azar appeared doubtful, but nodded.

Max opened the rear door. "I'll be back soon."

"But what do you want to eat?"

Max, already out of the car, bent down and grinned through the open doorway. "Surprise me. I trust you."

He closed the door and walked onto the footpath that ran around the marina. There were nine pontoons, each capable of mooring sixteen vessels. The smaller boats were closer to shore, while the larger ones were at the seaward end of the pontoons.

Max walked to the extreme left, then turned back and strolled along the rows of pontoons, pretending to be a tourist out sightseeing.

Each pontoon was accessed via a locked gate about six feet high, equipped with a smart card reader above the lock. A camera pointed at the footpath in front of the gate, while another focused down the pontoon. Max frowned; he had hoped to walk along the pontoons, but without an owner's key card, it didn't seem possible. On the gate was the letter A, and each berth was numbered, starting from one on the left side of the pontoon and nine on the right. He checked the property list saved on his phone. According to the list, Liam Mulroney's boat was berthed at I12. That was likely on the last pontoon, where the larger boats were moored.

Max continued walking slowly, working his way along the alphabet while eyeing the boats, playing the part of a boating enthusiast out for a stroll. Small sailing boats, a few sport fishing boats, and several catamarans occupied the nearest pontoons. As he walked further from the vehicle entrance, the boats grew larger. He kept walking, observing the boats but also scanning his surroundings for anything he could use to his advantage. The restaurants to his right gave way to marine supply stores and dive shops, and as he neared the end of the row, he spotted a wide boat ramp leading from the road into the water beside the last pontoon —Pontoon I.

He walked down the ramp until he reached the water's edge, gazing at the boats moored along the pontoon. Unlike the smaller boats earlier, these were larger, sleeker vessels, gleaming in the light of the setting sun. Counting off from the beginning, he spotted Liam Mulroney's boat four berths from the shore. The glossy black hull reflected the rippling waters of the lagoon, while the superstructure shone a brilliant white. It looked fast even while moored. Max knew little about luxury boats, but it certainly appeared expensive. The boat's windows were dark, and he turned to look back at the parked cars nearby. There was no sign of Liam Mulroney's G-Wagen. Frustration washed over him. So far, there had been no sign of the drug baron at any of the properties on his list, which meant he was hiding out elsewhere or had fled the country.

Max stood at the boat ramp, then glanced back at the fenced-off pontoon access. He knew what to do.

He grinned, feeling a surge of optimism at having a simple course of action.

If he didn't know where Liam was hiding, he would flush him out.

Turning, he walked back toward the Thai restaurant.

_____

22

Hakim slowed the car and turned into the driveway of his house. He switched off the engine and sat for a moment, staring at the front door. His daughter's pink bicycle, with tassels dangling from the handlebars, lay on its side near the bottom step. Through the sheers, he saw lights on inside, and glimpsed Latifah moving around, probably feeding Sariah and Aaliyah. His stomach churned, and he swallowed the acid rising in his throat.

It was unusual for him to be home this early. Normally, he didn't return until after dark, long after the girls had gone to bed. But today, he'd made excuses and left the office early. It had taken all his willpower to focus on work, but by the afternoon, he had given up. He had eaten little since the envelope had arrived, and his nerves were shot.

He glanced at the bouquet and the two soft toys on the passenger seat. He could never tell Latifah what he had done, but at least he could try to be a better husband—and a better father.

His phone buzzed in the cup holder. Muttering a curse,

he grabbed it, glanced at the screen, and cursed again, louder this time. Reluctantly, he answered the call.

"Did you forget something?" The Irish accent was unmistakable—Liam Mulroney. Hakim had never really noticed his accent before. Liam usually sounded more generically European. Now, it seemed much stronger, maybe because of the stress.

"Forgotten something?" Hakim repeated, momentarily confused. Then it clicked. "Oh, no, no... I was going to call you later. When I have something to report."

"Later? Later?" Liam growled. "I told you I want updates twice a day."

Hakim winced, rubbing his forehead while his eyes stayed on the house, watching his family inside. He needed to take control, at least of this situation. He couldn't completely bow to Liam Mulroney. Taking a steadying breath, he spoke with authority. "Liam, we both want the same thing. Someone out there is killing people, and they need to be behind bars. I've got my best men on this, and I'll let you know as soon as there's news. But right now, there's nothing. We only started the investigation today. These things take time."

"I don't have fucking time, Hakim!" Liam's voice thundered through the phone. "I want results."

Hakim closed his eyes and inhaled deeply before responding, "You'll get results, Liam. You always do with me. But you have to let it play out. Have I ever let you down?"

There was a long silence on the other end before Liam spoke again. "If I don't get results, those photos will go public."

The line went dead.

Hakim threw the phone onto the dashboard, exhaling sharply. *"Ibn kalb,"* he muttered.

He was doing everything he could to find out who was behind the shootout and the fire. That was his job. No matter whose property it was, he would have been working to lock up those responsible. He didn't need Liam's threats hanging over him to do his job. He was a good cop, no matter what his private life was like. Sure, he turned a blind eye to Liam's activities outside the city, and he was compensated for it. But when it came to public safety, he was uncompromising.

He picked up his phone again, found a number, and dialed.

"Sir?" a voice answered.

"All set?"

"Yes, sir. We'll start in about an hour."

"Good. Keep me posted."

"Yes, sir."

Hakim hung up, put the phone in his pocket, and stepped out of the car. Walking to the passenger side, he opened the door and picked up the bouquet and soft toys. Straightening up, he looked at the front door, taking a deep breath to steady himself. He pushed down the guilt gnawing at his insides. One more deep breath, a slow exhale, and then he walked toward the house. He was a good man, a loving husband, and a devoted father.

He opened the door.

"Baba!"

Hakim smiled and stepped inside.

23

Major Omar Al-Farsi stepped out of the elevator and paused in the lobby as two of his men followed behind. A tall, slim Eastern European woman stood behind a lectern at the entrance to the restaurant, her expression worried, unsure whether to speak.

Omar gave her a brief nod, sparing her the decision, then led his men through the entrance. Once inside, he scanned the tables. Several diners glanced up, curious about the three uniformed policemen. Despite being on the twentieth floor of a sleek skyscraper, the restaurant's wood-paneled walls and crystal chandeliers evoked the atmosphere of an upscale restaurant in Paris or Vienna. Soft classical music drifted through hidden speakers while waiters in crisp white shirts and black ties moved quietly between tables. It wasn't the kind of place a policeman like Major Omar could afford to visit on his salary.

"He's over there, sir," murmured Constable Hassan Al-Jaberi, nodding toward a table in the back.

Omar looked in that direction just as Stavros Nikolaidas

glanced up. A frown creased Stavros's face, his wine glass halting in mid-air. One of his two female companions noticed his reaction and turned to see who had caught his attention.

Stavros Nikolaidas was allegedly the largest supplier of MDMA in the Emirates... allegedly.

"Let's go," Omar muttered, leading the way through the tables. More diners noticed them now, conversations fading into a hush as they watched the trio move through the restaurant.

Out of the corner of his eye, Omar saw the restaurant manager hurrying toward him, but he waved him off with an irritated gesture. The manager stopped in his tracks and turned back toward the bar that ran along one side of the restaurant.

Stavros had set down his wineglass and was now watching their approach, both of his ring-covered hands flat on the table, a smirk on his fleshy face. His companions, both blonde, with exaggeratedly long false eyelashes, their surgically enhanced chests bursting out of the plunging necklines of their slinky cocktail dresses, turned in their seats to see what was happening. Omar couldn't help but think they wouldn't have looked out of place on the red carpet at the Oscars. He doubted they were with Stavros for his charm or conversation.

Reaching the table, Omar spoke in a low voice, "Stavros Nikolaidas, I need you to come with us."

Stavros sneered, glancing between Omar and the two constables. "Why?"

"We'll discuss that down at the station."

"Huh," Stavros scoffed, shaking his head. He looked at the women, then back at Omar. "As you can see, I'm having dinner with these lovely ladies. I suggest you turn around, take your guard dogs, and leave. Or should I call Colonel Hakim Al-Hamadi and express my displeasure?" His smile was cold, and Omar noticed his index finger tapping nervously on the white tablecloth.

Omar straightened up, speaking louder this time. "Colonel Al-Hamadi has requested you come to the station." He nodded to his men, who moved around the table to stand by Stavros's shoulder. "You can come quietly, or my men can assist you." Omar smiled back at him.

A flush spread over Stavros's face as he clenched his chubby hands into fists. He started to say something but stopped, realizing the entire restaurant was watching. His face reddened further. He drained his wine in one gulp, pushed back his chair, and tossed his napkin onto the table. With a grunt, he heaved himself to his feet, scowling. "I'll have your job," he growled.

"Whatever you say," Omar replied, gesturing toward the entrance. "After you."

Stavros muttered under his breath and stormed out of the restaurant, trailed by the two constables.

Omar turned to the two stunned women with a smile. "Good evening, ladies. Enjoy your meal." Then, he made his way out of the restaurant, nodding and smiling at the diners, who were still watching him leave.

24

"And they all lived happily ever after." Hakim closed the book with a flourish, grinning first at Aaliyah, then at Sariah.

"Read one more, *Baba*," Sariah begged.

"Yes, *Baba*, one more," Aaliyah echoed.

Hakim chuckled, leaned down, and kissed Aaliyah on the forehead. "It's time to sleep." He pulled the duvet up under her chin, tucking it in. "Sleep well, *habibti,*" he whispered.

He stood, noticing Latifah in the doorway, and winked at her before moving to Sariah's bed. He bent down, kissed her cheek, and said, "Good night, *habibti.*"

"Good night, *Baba*," she whispered, her eyes already closing. "Thank you for the unicorn."

Hakim smiled and adjusted the fluffy white unicorn beside her pillow. Then he stood and reached for the bedside lamp.

"No, no, leave it on," Aaliyah protested from the other bed.

Hakim smiled and nodded. "Okay, my *amira*, my princess."

He gazed at his daughters, his heart swelling with pride. They meant everything to him. A tear welled up, and he blinked it away before turning to the door. Latifah leaned against the frame, her eyes twinkling with a soft smile. He smiled back, stepping past her and gently closing the door.

"They're so happy you made it home for bedtime," Latifah whispered, wrapping her arms around his waist and resting her head on his shoulder. "So am I."

Guilt threatened to surface, but Hakim pushed it away, focusing instead on her warmth, the smell of her hair, the softness of her waist. He held her closer and kissed the top of her head. "So am I," he murmured, realizing how much he missed being here. The demands of his job had kept him away too often, missing family moments he could never get back.

Right now, with his daughters asleep and the woman he loved in his arms, he knew there was nowhere else he'd rather be. He closed his eyes, sinking into the comfort of her embrace, gently swaying from side to side. Latifah looked up at him after a moment, her dark eyes searching his face.

"Is everything okay?" she asked softly.

Hakim blinked, then forced a smile. Did she suspect something? "Yes, of course. Why?"

She shrugged, smiling. "Nothing, just asking. You're not always this... affectionate."

His smile faltered slightly. "I'm sorry. The job... you know how it is." He kissed her forehead. "I'll try harder." He gazed into her eyes, feeling the depth of his love for her. "I love you. Never forget that."

Latifah giggled. "I know you do."

He bent down, kissing her deeply, more passionately

than he had in months. His hand slid from her waist, squeezing her buttock, as a quiet moan escaped her lips. His pulse quickened, and desire stirred inside him. She pulled back slightly and whispered, "Not here." She nodded toward the girls' half-open bedroom door.

Hakim grinned, releasing her and following her down the hallway toward their own bedroom. He watched her nightgown sway over her hips, his breath quickening.

Suddenly, a buzzing in his pocket interrupted the moment. It took him a second to realize what it was. He grimaced, muttering a curse under his breath. Pulling out his phone, he glanced at the screen before looking up at Latifah. She stood in their doorway, a familiar look of disappointment on her face.

"I'm sorry," he said.

25

"Wait here."

"Okay," Azar replied, turning in his seat to look back at Max with concern.

Max winked. "Don't worry. Just pretend you're having a nap."

Azar swallowed, then looked around at the street outside. "Okay."

Max reached forward, gave his friend a reassuring squeeze on the shoulder, then opened the door and climbed out.

The temperature had dropped from the scorching heat of the day, but it was still in the low thirties centigrade and after the air-conditioned interior of the taxi it hit him like a blast from a hairdryer.

Max stood and checked his surroundings. The taxi was parked one block back from the marina, in a dark spot behind a row of trees. Behind it was a long warehouse, closed for the night, and on the opposite side of the now deserted road was a patch of water beyond which were the brightly lit and still busy dry docks.

Max had sat with Azar for several hours at the Thai restaurant, having a leisurely meal and chatting about life. But the whole time he'd kept an eye on the boat moored at Pontoon I. No-one came on or off and the boat remained dark. Satisfied it was empty, he had paid the bill and, after a brief visit to a hardware store and a clothes shop, gone back to the hotel with Azar for a few hours' rest.

Now at three am, he was back, dressed in black running shorts, a loose black t-shirt, a baseball cap pulled low over his face and a pair of lightweight sandals. Around his waist was a small waterproof pouch containing a toolkit, a set of lock picks, a pocket knife, and a penlight.

He left the taxi behind, walking casually down the deserted road before turning into the marina. The cafés and restaurants were shuttered and dark, not a soul in sight. Max stayed on the restaurant side of the street, deliberately keeping away from the cameras mounted above the floodlit gates leading to each pontoon. His steps were unhurried, casual, as if he were simply out for a late-night stroll. If anyone asked, he'd say he couldn't sleep and needed some sea air.

A faint breeze drifted through, carrying a hint of salt from the sea. The distant hum of machinery and the faint smell of diesel wafted over from the docks. Max kept walking, his eyes constantly scanning the area, alert for any signs of danger.

At the end of the row of restaurants stood a dimly lit guard hut, the guard fast asleep, his chin slumped on his chest. He wasn't even aware of Max walking past.

Max neared the slipway, took one more casual glance around, then crossed the road and headed down to the water's edge. The dim streetlights barely reached the end of the slipway, leaving him in near darkness. The only sound was the gentle lapping of water against the concrete. He stood there for a moment, listening, making sure he was truly alone. Satisfied, he waded into the water. When it reached his waist, he began swimming.

It wasn't far—maybe fifty meters at most—but Max swam slowly, careful not to splash or make any sudden movements. The water was warm but smelled strongly of petroleum products, and he made sure not to let any get into his mouth. He felt secure that no one would spot him; his head was just a small, dark shape bobbing in the water, and there was no one around to notice. As he reached the bow of the boat, he swam around to the seaward side, out of range of the onshore cameras, then made his way to the stern.

Reaching the swim platform, he gripped it with his fingertips and paused, listening again while catching his breath, gathering himself for what came next. His eyes landed on the silver letters across the glossy black hull at the rear of the boat: 'High Seas.' Max smirked. Liam Mulroney, it seemed, had a sense of humor.

Once Max had his breathing under control, he hoisted himself up onto the swim platform, careful not to make a sound. He paused, listening intently to see if his movement had been detected. The yacht was big enough that his added weight didn't disturb it, and there was barely a ripple. He stayed crouched for a moment, allowing the water to drain off his body before pushing himself to his feet and, bending double, crept up the steps from the swim platform to the afterdeck. He reached for the handle, testing it gently. Locked. That confirmed his suspicion—the yacht was unoc-cupied, just as he had hoped.

Max knelt, unzipped the pack strapped around his waist, and retrieved his lock picks. The last time he'd used them had been on the West Bank, outside a house under the cover of night. He hoped the muscle memory hadn't faded.

Inserting the tension wrench, he turned it slightly to apply pressure on the lock plug, then inserted a 'city rake', easing it up and down, back and forth, feeling for the pins, until with a click the driven pins slipped into place and the door unlocked. It had taken Max less than twenty seconds. Pleased that his skills hadn't diminished, he stowed his tools and slid the door open just enough to enter and slipped inside.

Once inside, he closed the door behind him and paused, letting his eyes adjust to the dim light. The salon was spacious, furnished with cream leather L-shaped sofas on either side, leading to a galley on the left and a dining area on the right. Ahead, near the bow, was the helm station, and a staircase descending to the lower deck.

Max moved quietly across the salon and descended the stairs, pulling out his penlight once he reached the lower level. A quick sweep of the beam revealed a cabin in the bow, and two single berth cabins on either side of the passageway. At the rear was the main cabin, a luxuriously appointed bedroom that took up the entire width of the boat. It had a flatscreen television on a table at the end of the bed and a full-sized bathroom with shower, w/c and bidet. Max had a cursory look around, but finding nothing of interest, made his way back upstairs.

He again stood for a moment looking around, then made his way aft, slipping out the rear door onto the deck. Max had studied plans of the yacht while back in his hotel and he located the hatch in the aft deck that allowed access into the engine room. Lifting the hatch, he climbed down the ladder before pulling the hatch closed above him. Only then did he turn his pen light back on.

26

Max stooped in the engine compartment, the space barely accommodating his frame. He had to angle his head sideways to avoid banging it against the roof.

The information Max had found online had been of little help in terms of the engine layout, and as he shone his flashlight around, the beam bouncing off the engine and electrical components, sweat beaded on his forehead and his heart rate increased. He was running against the clock and had to finish his work before someone noticed the tampering or the boat began to sink.

His first thought had been to set fire to the yacht, but the difficulty was setting fire to the diesel fuel on board. Diesel was not as flammable as petrol and would take more than a tossed match or lighter. He could have used the liquor in the bar, just as he'd done in Caim Mulroney's villa, but a fire would be spotted quickly and he still needed to make his escape through the water and back to the taxi. After considerable thought and research, he had settled on scuttling the boat.

Locating the fusebox, he studied the maze of switches, then, deciding not to waste time, flicked them all to the off position. He traced the wiring from the fusebox to the battery compartment. As he opened it, the beam of his flashlight revealed the battery banks. Spotting the isolation switches, he turned them to off and began disconnecting the cables, first the negative, then the positive.

Max paused, his breath coming in quick, shallow bursts. Satisfied that the electrical systems had all been disabled, he then searched the engine compartment for the sea cocks, the valves that controlled the entry and exit of water into the boat. His eyes flicked to a hatch on the floor, a spot he had overlooked earlier. Opening the hatch, he located two of the valves and turned the first lever counterclockwise to open it. He'd read that if the valves were left open, and the bilge pumps were inoperative, it would only be a matter of time before the engine room would start filling up with water. The second valve seemed to be jammed, and he cursed under his breath as he struggled to turn it. The valve finally gave way with a grating squeal, and he turned it counter-clockwise.

There was a faint sound of water beginning to trickle in as he knelt and watched. Would it be fast enough?

He stood and continued his search for any more sea cocks and found another two. One appeared to be linked to a generator and the second, he guessed, was for the air-conditioner cooling. He opened those too and then took a last look around the engine compartment. Satisfied that his sabotage was working, he moved quickly but quietly up the ladder and cautiously opened the hatch. With his senses on high alert, he looked around, listening, and then, sure he was alone, climbed out and closed the hatch behind him.

Slipping down to the swim platform, Max's gaze fell on

the power cable running from the boat to the pier. He yanked it out, severing the connection to the shore power, then slipped back into the water with barely a splash, his movements smooth and deliberate. The water felt cool against his sweat soaked skin, a welcome relief after the stuffy, enclosed engine room.

He only hoped he had done enough.

27

L iam Mulroney sat at his desk in his villa in Muscat, the early morning light creeping in through the heavy drapes. The room, adorned with antique teak and mahogany furniture and paintings from contemporary Omani and African artists, usually luxurious and comforting, seemed cold and unwelcoming today. Fatigue etched Liam's face, his eyes bloodshot from a sleepless night spent wrestling with the ghosts of the attack on his Dubai villa. The vivid memories of that night—the gunfire, the chaos, death—haunted him relentlessly.

Barry leaned against the opposite wall, his arms crossed. A heavy silence hung in the room. The two men had been working through the night, trying to piece together who could have been behind such a brutal assault. Despite their efforts, they were no further forward. Those they could get hold of knew nothing, but even more worrying was that many didn't even bother to answer their calls.

Liam had always held everything together. He prided himself on being in control, on being the one who dictated terms, never at the mercy of others. Every deal, every negotiation, every violent confrontation had been a testament to his strength and strategic mind.

Yet, he had failed.

He clenched his jaw, fighting back the anger and grief that threatened to overwhelm him.

The buzzing of his phone jolted him from his thoughts. The caller ID read 'Marina Manager.' His heart skipped a beat. He knew it was more bad news, there being no other reason the manager would call him so early in the morning.

"Yes?"

"Mr Mulroney?" The manager's voice was hesitant, apologetic. "I'm... I'm sorry to inform you that your boat, the 'High Seas,' has sunk."

Liam felt as if he'd been punched in the gut. He'd loved his boat almost as much as his Aston Martin, but it had been more than just a luxury; it was a key asset in his operations. He used it often to wine and dine those he did business with. Its sinking was a major blow and surely couldn't be a coincidence. The timing was too convenient. Liam's hands gripped the edge of his desk, his knuckles turning white. He felt violated, as if someone had reached into his world and taken a piece.

He stood abruptly, his chair scraping noisily against the floor, and handed the phone to Barry.

"The boat," was all he could say.

Barry took the phone and began questioning the manager while Liam paced the room. He could feel his anger boiling over, a fierce, searing heat burning in his gut, as the room closed in around him. The polished surfaces and opulent furnishings, which had once represented his success, now felt like a cruel mockery.

Barry ended the call and before he could say anything, Liam growled, his voice low but laced with fury, "This is unacceptable. First, my home. Now, my boat. Whoever is behind this is destroying everything I've built."

Barry nodded and looked down at the phone in his hand.

"We have to find out who's behind this and make them pay," Liam continued.

Barry grunted agreement.

Liam's mind raced. How had everything changed so quickly? Every step of his journey, from the rough neighborhoods of Belfast to the luxurious surroundings of Dubai, had been marked by his unwavering control. He had built his empire with blood, sweat, and an iron will. But now, as he stood in his villa, surrounded by the trappings of his success, he felt a creeping sense of helplessness.

Barry's voice broke through his reverie. "What do you want to do next?"

Liam took a deep breath, forcing himself to focus. He would use his anger, his sense of violation, as fuel. Someone had made a grave mistake in underestimating him. He would hunt them down and make them pay for every ounce of damage they had inflicted. And in doing so, he would reassert his control over the empire he had fought so hard to build. "Use every resource we have to track them down, Barry. We'll make sure they suffer so much no-one will ever think of crossing me again."

28

H akim lay in bed beside his wife, the slow and steady rise and fall of her chest in complete contrast to the turmoil in his mind. The morning light, soft and golden, filtered through the curtains, casting gentle patterns across the room. It should have been a peaceful start to the day, but the thought of what lay ahead pressed heavily on him.

Latifah had been asleep by the time he had finished his calls last night and he had crept into bed, lying silently beside her, letting her sleep.

His men had done well, rounding up the main kingpins in the drug trade and bringing them in for questioning. They had faced indignation, veiled threats, and, in some cases, outright abuse, but everyone on the list Liam had given them had been rounded up and were now waiting in the cells at the station. He had told Omar to hold them overnight. These men were used to a life of luxury and there was nothing like a night in a cold, hard cell to soften someone up.

The day promised to be grueling. Extracting the information he needed while preserving his authority, and his job was a fine line to tread. There was no knowing who they were connected to and what the potential repercussions could be. They all knew the authorities turned a blind eye as long as they weren't too overt in their criminal activities, but if he pushed too far, it could prod them into calling in favours and getting him removed.

Hakim's gaze remained fixed on the ceiling, his anxiety and apprehension growing with every minute. His phone buzzed softly on the bedside table, breaking the uneasy quiet. He picked it up and glanced at the screen.

Mulroney.

With a weary sigh, he carefully slid out of bed, making sure not to wake Latifah. The marble floor, cooled by the air-conditioning, sent a chill through his bare feet as he crossed the room. He shut the bathroom door behind him with a soft click and answered the call, bracing himself for the worst.

"Hakim," Liam Mulroney barked without preamble.

"What's happened?" he asked, striving to keep his voice steady, though his mind was already racing with dread.

"My boat," Mulroney's voice seethed with barely contained rage, "it's sunk. I want to know how this happened and who's responsible."

Hakim's thoughts raced. Was it an accident or was it another attack? "I'll need more details," Hakim said, forcing calm into his tone. "When did this occur? Where is the boat now?"

"Early this morning," Mulroney snapped. "It was moored at the Port Saeed Marina. Now, it's lying at the bottom of the bay."

Hakim cleared his throat. "Okay. Are you sure it's not just an accident?"

"Are you fucking stupid?"

Hakim winced and held the phone away from his ear as Liam roared down the phone.

"Of course it's not a fucking accident. The boat was tied up in the marina. There was no storm. It wasn't at sea. How the fuck do you think it sank?"

Hakim's jaw tightened. Few people dared speak to him in that tone of voice. But he remembered the photographs and forced himself to remain calm.

"I understand," Hakim said, maintaining his authoritative tone despite Liam's anger. "I'll dispatch a team to the marina right away to assess the damage. In the meantime, if you have any further information about any threats or suspicious activities related to the boat, it would be helpful."

"If I have any information? If I have any information?" Mulroney repeated. "You're the fucking cop! Fix this, Hakim. And quickly."

The call ended abruptly, leaving Hakim staring at his reflection in the bathroom mirror. He took a deep breath, steadying himself. Returning to the bedroom, he carefully adjusted the covers around his wife. She slept soundly, her thick black hair spread out like a halo around her on the pillow, thankfully unaware of the storm brewing in Hakim's life.

He took a deep breath, retrieved his watch from the side table and picked up his uniform from the chair on which he had discarded it during the night. With one last glance back at his sleeping wife, he slipped silently out of the bedroom. After dressing quickly in the spare bedroom, splashing water on his face and taming his hair, he left the house in the same clothes he had arrived in. As he reversed his car out onto the street, he called Major Omar.

The interrogations would have to wait.

M ax's eyes blinked open. It was pitch dark. For a second he was puzzled, then remembered where he was. He turned his head to look at the digital clock on the bedside table. 9:30 AM. He had been asleep for about five hours... not nearly enough... but as the memory of the night's activities came flooding back, he knew he wouldn't be able to sleep anymore.

He climbed out of bed, stood and stretched in the darkness before making his way over to the window and pulling back the curtains, allowing a flood of bright sunlight to fill the room. Blinking rapidly, he raised his arm to shield his eyes from the sun. He could already feel the heat through the window and once his eyes adjusted, he turned back to the view. The fireboat had long since left the lagoon and steam and smoke had stopped rising from the destroyed villa across on The Palm. If you didn't look too closely, it was as if nothing had happened.

He turned and walked over to the connecting door between the two rooms and cracked it open. Before he saw anything, he could hear Azar snoring loudly in the dark room, and he chuckled before closing the door again. Let him sleep. He had stayed faithfully waiting for Max to return, and Max doubted he had got any rest in the taxi. He didn't need Azar right now, and neither had got enough sleep in the last few days.

Max crossed the room, picked up the television remote, and flicked on the television. Flipping through the channels, he searched for a local news station to check if his sabotage had been successful and made the local news.

He found one in Arabic and he sat on the end of the bed and watched. The broadcast was filled with mundane updates and with a growing sense of disappointment Max was about to give up when, about fifteen minutes in, the news reader mentioned a significant marine incident. He leaned forward and turned up the volume as the anchor described a yacht named 'High Seas' that had sunk at the Port Saeed Marina. A brief clip flashed on the screen showing the partially submerged motor yacht, the superstructure just visible above the pontoon, while several emergency vessels floated around it. The news was brief, but confirmed his work had been successful. No immediate suspects were mentioned, but a police spokesman was quoted as saying the matter was 'under investigation.'

Max turned off the TV and stared at the now-blank screen, his mind racing. He had just sent two million euros of Liam Mulroney's fortune to the bottom of the harbor, a move that would undoubtedly enrage the Irishman. Max grinned, but he knew this was only the beginning. The yacht had been his first target because it was movable—if he'd waited, Liam could have moved it somewhere safe. But the real estate? That was immovable, and Max would keep hitting Liam's properties until he forced him out of hiding.

His stomach growled, pulling him from his thoughts. He

glanced at the clock. Breakfast seemed like a good next step before diving into the day's plans. He picked up the phone and ordered room service, then headed to the bathroom for a quick shower.

Fifteen minutes later, freshly showered and dressed, Max heard a knock at the door. He opened it to find a room service cart laden with breakfast for two. After signing the bill and handing over a generous tip, Max sent the waiter on his way, just as there was another knock—this time from the connecting door.

Max walked over and opened it to find a disheveled Azar standing in the doorway, wrapped in a bathrobe. His eyes were bleary with sleep, stubble shadowed his chin, and his hair sticking up in wild tufts.

"Sleep well?" Max asked with a grin. "Come, I've ordered breakfast."

"How are you so bright in the morning?" Azar muttered, rubbing the sleep from his eyes.

Max grinned and shrugged. "It's a beautiful day. Look outside."

Azar frowned at the window, then looked back at Max with confusion.

Max grinned wider, then stood to one side and gestured toward the room service cart over by the table. "Come on in."

Azar shuffled past in his hotel slippers and stopped by the cart, staring at the cloches and the jug of orange juice, clearly still half asleep.

"Help yourself, my friend," Max said, pouring a glass of juice and holding it out to Azar.

"Thank you," Azar replied, taking the glass and sitting down. Max poured himself a coffee, then lifted the cloches to reveal scrambled eggs and beef bacon. The smell filled the room, making his stomach rumble with anticipation.

"I'm so hungry," Max muttered, spooning a generous portion of eggs onto his plate before sitting down opposite Azar.

Azar, however, remained quiet, absently sipping his orange juice, his eyes distant as he stared at the table.

Max raised an eyebrow. "You didn't sleep properly? I heard you snoring like a steam train."Azar looked up. "When do we know if it worked?"

Max chewed his mouthful of bacon and swallowed. "It worked. It's on the news already."

"Oh." Azar perked up, a smile on his face for the first time. "That's good." He put down his juice and reached for a plate. "So what happens next?"

Max chewed thoughtfully, his mind drifting to the list of Liam's properties. He needed to decide on the next target. Ideally, it would be the most valuable, but he had to avoid civilian casualties, which meant staying away from the apartments. The villas were an option, but the commercial buildings would hit Liam where it hurt the most. Max figured a nighttime strike would be the best approach, ensuring the staff wouldn't be around.

He glanced up at Azar, who was quietly spooning food onto his plate, his gaze occasionally flicking over to Max, clearly waiting for an answer. Max knew he needed transport, but was hesitant to involve his friend any further. Then he remembered the Range Rover he'd taken from Liam's men. It was still sitting in the hotel car park. That would do nicely, but first, he had other tasks to handle.

"What happens next, Azar, is we finish our breakfast, and then I need to do some shopping."

30

"What would make a boat this size sink like this?" Hakim asked.

There was no immediate answer, and he turned to look at the marina manager, a tall Dutchman with a deep tan and floppy blond hair.

Realising Hakim was looking at him, he shrugged. "I don't know. Could be...." he trailed off, his eyes going back to the partially submerged hull of the 'High Seas.'

Hakim frowned deeply, not taking his eyes off the man, who looked as if a prized pet had died. "Dirk, is that right?"

Dirk nodded forlornly.

"Could be what, Dirk?"

Dirk took a deep breath, his shoulders rising and falling, then he turned and faced Hakim. He shook his head and exhaled loudly. "I honestly don't know how this happened. It's a newish boat, only seven years old. Well maintained. The weather was calm." He shook his head again. "It doesn't make sense."

"Well, something must have happened."

Dirk screwed up his face and turned back to look at the boat, his hands on his hips.

Hakim studied him. He must have been in his early thirties, although deep lines around his eyes from squinting against the sun made him look older. He looked fit, well muscled calves poking out from a pair of baggy cargo shorts suggesting he was a runner. Dirk reached up and pulled the brightly coloured Oakleys perched on his head over his eyes.

"Maybe... maybe, I mean I've seen it happen once before... maybe the crew left the sea cocks open by mistake?"

"Sea cocks?" Hakim shot a glance at Major Omar, who was standing on the other side of Dirk. "What are they?"

"Well, they allow water in and out to cool the engine, to flush the toilets, even to cool the air-conditioning."

Hakim's frown deepened. "Look, I know nothing about boats, so explain it to me like I'm a beginner."

"Well," Dirk turned to face Hakim. "There are two elements. Sea cocks are valves that control the water flow into and out of the boat. Think of them like a faucet. They are necessary for various functions, as I've already mentioned."

"Okay," Hakim nodded and glanced at Omar to make sure he was taking notes.

"The other element are the bilge pumps. These are like an emergency water remover. Any water that collects in the lowest part of the boat, the bilge, gets removed by the bilge pumps. It should all happen automatically."

"So if the sea cocks are left open, the bilge pumps will pump any water out?"

"Exactly."

Hakim turned to look at the boat. "So, how did this happen?"

Dirk turned to look at the boat, too. "Well, the bilge pump must have stopped working. It must have a fault."

"Is that common?"

He shook his head. "No, but it can happen. That's one reason the sea cocks are closed when the boat is moored."

Hakim pursed his lips and looked around. On shore there was a small crowd of onlookers, drawn no doubt by the news reports. A police RIB floated between the bow of the 'High Seas' and the boat slip, just in case anyone was tempted to come closer, and a constable stood by the entrance to the pontoon keeping sightseers out.

He turned back to Dirk. "So, how do we find out?"

"We have to refloat the boat."

"How long would that take?"

Dirk puffed out his cheeks and shrugged. "A couple of days? A week? It depends on the insurers."

"A week?" Hakim shook his head. "Too long. I need to know now."

Dirk looked puzzled. He opened his mouth to ask why, then under the force of Hakim's glare, obviously thought better of it.

"Um, well, we could send in a diver. He might find out what happened."

Hakim nodded. "Good." He looked at Omar. "Get it done asap. Then meet me back at the station."

He turned on his heel and strode back down the pontoon toward the shore. He had a bunch of drug dealers to interrogate.

31

M ax's phone buzzed while he was browsing the shelves of a hardware store. He glanced at the screen, then put it to his ear.

"Any news?"

"Yes," Ramesh replied. "Can you come over? I'd rather not talk on the phone."

Max turned his wrist and looked at his watch. "I'll be there in an hour."

An hour later, Max stood looking up at the camera, waiting for Ramesh to buzz him in. He had asked Azar to drop him off and then sent him back to the hotel with the supplies he had bought for the next phase of the plan.

The door clicked open and Max made his way down the corridor, through the intervening doors, and into what he now thought of as Ramesh's dungeon.

His nose twitched at the smell of stale air and takeaway food, and once again he thanked his stars he had never been interested in computers. Ramesh was still in the same clothes he was wearing when Max had left him the previous day. Max cast his eye over the unwashed coffee cups and the empty food cartons and asked, "Have you been here since I left?"

Ramesh grunted, then turned around in his chair, stretched his legs, and clasped his hands behind his head.

Ignoring Max's question, he said, "I've found something very interesting."

Max nodded. "What?"

"Your man has been making regular payments to a numbered account in the Cayman Islands."

Max frowned, not sure how that helped him.

Ramesh was grinning. "I worked out who the account belongs to."

"Who?"

Ramesh released his hands, sat forward, and turned his chair to look at the monitor in front of him. "Colonel Hakim Al-Hamadi, currently stationed at the Al Barsha Police station."

Max walked forward and stood beside him. "How did you find that out? The whole purpose of a numbered account is that it doesn't have a name on it."

Ramesh grinned even wider. "Well, I found an encrypted folder labelled H. It took me a while to crack it open, but when I did, I discovered a record of the payments. Every month on the third of the month going back three years."

"Okay."

"In the same folder was a sub-folder containing a series of photographs. Photographs of an Arab-looking man having..." Ramesh coughed, "sexual relations with women."

Max nodded slowly. "The cop?"

"Yes!" Ramesh exclaimed. "Don't you want to know how I identified him?"

"How did you identify him?" Max humoured him.

"I ran his face through a facial recognition program I designed, which searches the internet and matches the image with others online."

"And it matches the Colonel."

"Exactly!" Ramesh clapped his hands together in delight.

Max turned and rested his butt against the workstation. He folded his arms and looked down at his feet while he thought. "So we have payments to the cop and we also have photos of the cop having sex."

"He's married with two kids," Ramesh interjected.

"So he's being paid, but also blackmailed."

Ramesh nodded. "That's what it looks like."

"Carrot and the stick," Max muttered.

"What do you mean?"

"You offer him a choice. Work for you and get paid. Say no and you release the photos." Max sniffed. "Huh."

"Clever," Ramesh commented.

"Hmmmm," Max thought about what he could do with the information. He wasn't sure yet, nothing immediately springing to mind.

"Did you find out where Mulroney is yet?"

"No idea." Ramesh nodded at the monitor. "The cop might know."

Max pursed his lips. Ramesh could be right, but he wasn't about to rock up at the police station to ask the whereabouts of Liam Mulroney from a corrupt cop.

"Okay. Text me what you have on this guy. I'll have a think about what I can do."

Ramesh nodded. "Done." He tilted his head to the side, a mischievous look on his face. "You look tired. Been up all night?"

Max shook his head and shrugged. "Just been busy."

"Yeah, well, I guess we're all in the same boat." Ramesh winked.

32

M ax rolled up to the kerb in the black Range Rover Sport, doused the lights and rolled down the windows before turning the engine off. He reclined the seat slightly and settled in for a couple of hours of observation.

He had left a clearly disappointed Azar behind, not wanting to get him too involved in criminal activities. Azar had a family to support and Max didn't feel comfortable about putting him in harm's way if it could be avoided.

So he'd taken the Range Rover he'd seized from Caim's men, driven it to a supermarket car park and swapped out the number plates with another vehicle. He wasn't sure if the police were looking for it, but didn't want to take a chance. It was a comfortable car with great visibility, plenty of power, and four-wheel drive if he needed it. And in a city where luxury cars were everywhere, it didn't stick out too much.

A soft breeze blew warm air off the desert, but Max preferred to keep the windows down and the air conditioning off. That way, he could listen to the sounds of the night and notice if anything wasn't as it should be.

Diagonally opposite him about two hundred meters away was a warehouse owned by one of Liam Mulroney's legitimate companies, Atlas Regional Trading FZCO. Ostensibly, it traded in foodstuffs throughout the Middle East and North Africa. But although legitimate and profitable, it served another purpose. Hidden within the shipments was the real source of Liam Mulroney's wealth. Captagon pills for Saudi Arabia, Tramadol for the Egyptians, and MDMA for the partygoers in Israel and Lebanon.

The front of the building was well lit, a floodlight on each end lighting up the facade and the empty parking lot at the front. Empty, that is, except for a battered white pickup, which Max assumed belonged to the security guard in the guard hut beside the fence. A high chain-link fence surrounded the building and an equally high gate on rollers blocked entry to the carpark. But that didn't worry Max. He had a plan.

He turned his wrist to check the time on the luminous dial of his G-Shock—just after midnight. Still time. He glanced in the mirrors, surveying his surroundings. The other buildings were as quiet as ever, and the street was deserted except for a tractor-trailer parked a few hundred meters behind him in the dirt off the side of the road. The air was still, broken only by the distant sound of the motorway, its hum carrying on the breeze.

Reaching for the binoculars on the seat beside him, he focused them on the guard hut. The guard, an elderly man, bearded but balding, was eating and watching something on a screen. Max adjusted the focus. Judging by the speed of movement of the images on the screen, the guard had replaced the security footage with a movie. Max grinned and put the binoculars down again. He would give him a couple of hours. Allow the food and boredom to take effect.

33

Hakim leaned his elbows on his desk and buried his face in his hands. It had been a long day. The sun had long since set and the day shift replaced by the night shift, but he still had one more call to make before going home.

He placed the palms of his hands flat on the desk, on either side of his cell phone, and took a deep breath. He wasn't looking forward to it. His eyes fell on the framed photo of Latifah and the girls, giggling and smiling at the camera. He remembered taking the photo. They had been on a family holiday to Euro-Disney in Paris. Just a year ago, but it felt like a lifetime. He sighed. Once this was all over, and providing he got out of it intact, he would take them away again. Latifah had never seen snow. Maybe he'd take them to Switzerland, to Zurich and the Matterhorn?

But first he had to deal with Liam Mulroney.

Picking up the phone, he pressed redial. As it rang out, he noticed something he hadn't picked up on before. The dial tone was different, longer, not the short double tones of a local call. Which meant only one thing. Liam was not in Dubai. Hakim frowned. So where was he?

Before he could think about it any more, Liam's voice growled down the phone.

"You'd better have some feckin good news!"

Hakim grimaced. Liam sounded more and more Irish each time he spoke to him.

He exhaled, wondering where he should start.

"Well?"

"The boat...the ahh 'High Seas.' It appears to have been an act of sabotage."

"Oi feckin told ya!" Liam exclaimed.

Hakim nodded as if Liam could see him. "Yes, well, we sent a diver in, and discovered that the electrical equipment had been tampered with, disabling the bilge system. The sea cocks were all in the open position, allowing water to enter the hull and with the bilge pumps deactivated, there was no way for the water to exit the hull."

Hakim heard Liam muttering to someone in the background. The conversation wasn't clear, but then he recognised the word Barry. He made a mental note that Liam wasn't alone.

"So, who did it?"

"We don't know yet."

"You don't know? Any eye witnesses? What about the marina security? Jesus, Mary, Mother of God! I pay a fortune to keep my boat there. The guard must have seen something. There's feckin' cameras everywhere!"

Hakim pushed back his chair and stood up. He moved over to the window and gazed out over the floodlit police station carpark.

"We've checked the camera footage for the entire night. We estimate the boat was sabotaged in the early hours of the morning. But no-one accessed the mooring from the shore after midnight."

"So what about before that? Do I have to do your job for you, you bloody eejit?"

Hakim gritted his teeth, his fingers tightening their grip on the phone. He wasn't sure what an 'eejit' was, but he could guess. "We checked that too. Everyone can be accounted for."

"So how the devil did they sink it? Because it sure as hell didn't sink itself."

Hakim took a deep breath, his eyes on a metallic blue Rolls Royce Cullinan that had just rolled into the carpark.

"Our guess is they accessed the boat from the seaward side. Unfortunately, there are no cameras on that side."

"Jeesus!"

The driver of the Cullinan, a beefy-looking man in a dark safari suit, climbed out and ran around to the passenger side, opened the door and stood waiting.

"So you're telling me, that in one of the 'safest'..." Liam emphasised the word, "cities in the world, someone shoots up my villa, sets it on fire, and then sinks my yacht, and you guys have no clue who did any of it?"

Hakim clenched his fist, then relaxed it. "We are making every enquiry, and we will get to the bottom of it." He leaned forward to get a better look at the Rolls Royce. The driver stood to attention as the corpulent form of Stavros Niko-laidas waddled out of the station and climbed into the back. Hakim allowed himself a small feeling of satisfaction. He was the last of the drug kingpins to leave, and just like the others, the slug of a man was not at all happy about spending a day and a night in the police station. Hakim would have loved to have kept them longer, but there were limits to how much even he could stretch his authority.

Liam had said something, but Hakim hadn't registered, his attention on the scene below. He had to regain some control of the conversation. He was a Police Colonel after all and needed to retain some dignity.

Interupting Liam, he said, "Today we questioned several suspects, people we thought were the most likely to ahh.... want to take control of your...business."

"And?"

"So far, nothing."

"Nothing? Nothing? For fuck's sake Hakim, sometimes I wonder what I'm paying you for!"

Hakim took a deep breath, trying to control his anger. As much as he disliked the man, he had to keep him on side. The last thing he needed was for Liam to send his wife the photographs.

"Liam, we're doing everything we can. But it will take time."

"I don't have time, Hakim. I want to come back and resume my life."

Hakim sensed an opportunity. "Come back? Why, where are you now?"

There was silence for a while and then, "Just find out who's behind this, Hakim. And make sure in your report that you say I had nothing to do with my boat sinking. That's two million euros sitting on the bottom of the harbour, and I don't want the insurance company to give me any trouble."

The line went dead before Hakim could reply.

34

L iam walked over to the sideboard and picked up the decanter. He glanced over at Barry and raised an eyebrow, and Barry replied with a nod. Liam poured three fingers of Jameson 18 into two crystal tumblers and then walked back to his desk. Barry half rose in his seat to take a glass from him, then sat down and nursed it in two hands while he waited for Liam.

Liam took a sniff from the top of the glass and then a large mouthful, draining almost half the contents in one go. He gulped it down before taking a seat, leaning back in the leather chesterfield, the glass resting in his lap.

"I loved that boat," Liam muttered after a while.

Barry nodded and took a sip of whiskey, rolling the liquid around in his mouth before swallowing.

Liam looked up and studied his friend's face. Thick stubble tinged with grey now covered his jaw, his hair lank and greasy, dark smudges of exhaustion under his eyes. Liam hadn't looked in the mirror since the morning, but he assumed he looked the same. Both of them were running on fumes. Stress, adrenaline, and copious amounts of strong coffee were the only thing keeping them going.

"We need to regain control, Barry. We can't assume Hakim and the Keystone Cops are going to shut this down for us."

"Yeah," Barry grunted.

Liam stared at him for a long moment, then asked, "What are you thinking?"

Barry shrugged. "To be honest…. nothing right now. I hate to say it, boss, but I'm beat."

Liam nodded. He hadn't seen Barry look so down-hearted for a very long time. He usually knew what to do in any situation, but this was the first time he had seen him looking defeated.

"Yeah. I know." Liam raised his glass to his lips and tossed back the contents, swallowing them down with a satisfied smack of his lips.

He reached for Barry's glass, "get that down you, and I'll top you up. There's not much more we can do tonight."

Barry shook his head. "I'll get it." He stood and reached for Liam's glass, just as Liam's phone began buzzing on the desk.

Liam handed the glass over, then picked up the phone and looked at the screen. He shook his head and sneered. "The vultures are circling," he muttered, then answered the call.

"Stavros. To what do I owe the pleasure?"

"Liam Mulroney. I hear you are in a spot of trouble."

"Not at all, Stavros, not at all. What makes you think that?"

Stavros chuckled. "Perhaps it was the fire at your villa, the dead bodies, and your boat springing a leak."

"An unfortunate series of accidents, Stavros."

"Cut the crap, Liam. I've just spent twenty-four hours in the Al Barsha Police station being questioned about the attacks on your property." Stavros' volume was rising, and Liam switched the phone to speaker mode and laid it on the table in front of him. "Twenty-four hours, Liam! Have you ever been to that station? Do you know what it's like?" Stavros continued, almost shouting now.

Liam caught Barry's eye and grimaced.

"I'm sorry Stavros, but look on the bright side. It will make you more appreciative of your current lifestyle," Liam joked, trying to make light of the situation.

"It's not a fucking joke, Liam," Stavros growled. "They picked me up from my table in Le Mistral. Three of them, Liam. Three *batsi*. People are talking. My reputation is destroyed."

"Your reputation?" Liam was about to make a scathing comment. He knew exactly what Stavros did for a living. But he erred on the side of caution. "That must have been very uncomfortable."

"What I want to know, Liam, is why the *batsi* came for me. I'm a legitimate businessman. Have you been telling tales?"

Liam shook his head and rolled his eyes at Barry, who had returned to the table with the refilled glasses. "First Stavros, everyone knows you're not a legitimate business-man, even the.... what do you call them.... *batsi*? The cops? You're kidding yourself if you think your attempts at being an honest businessman are fooling them." Liam paused and took a sip of his drink. "Second, if you ever suggest I'm a rat," he leaned forward until his mouth was just over the phone, "I'll come over and personally slit your fucking throat!"

There was silence for a while and then a quieter Stavros

spoke, "You're right, Liam. I spoke out of turn. But what I will say is this. You are poison right now. You've brought too much attention on yourself, and I don't want to be a part of it. I've already spent too much time in police company. I'm not about to spend any more."

Liam said nothing verbally, but the expression on his face said it all. His grip on his glass tightened, his knuckles turning white, a slight tremor causing the surface of the whiskey to ripple. He fought to regain control of his temper, but before he could say anything, Stavros spoke again.

"I've said nothing to the cops. I've even denied knowing anything about you. Whatever you need to do, I won't stand in your way, but from now on, you keep me out of it. I don't know you."

The phone went dead.

Liam hurled the glass across the room. It hit the drapes, splashing whiskey all over them before bouncing onto the carpet and rolling into the corner.

"Mother-fucking greasy wog son of a bitch!" he spat, then thumped the table with his fist. "I gave him the contacts to start, the ungrateful fucker. He buys his Molly from Pieter, for God's sake. Pieter! My feckin' guy."

Barry said nothing, just watching Liam with narrowed eyes, letting him rant. After a moment, he pushed his untouched glass of whiskey across the desk to Liam. Liam grabbed it and took a large mouthful, then sat back, shaking his head.

Barry stood and walked back to the sideboard to get a fresh glass. He poured himself a generous measure, then turned back just as the phone buzzed again.

"Oh, for fuck's sake," Liam groaned. "What is it now?"

He picked up the phone and looked at the screen. "Jeesus, now it's feckin' Sharif!"

35

I t was two am when Max picked up the binoculars for the last time and glassed the warehouse. He had been in the car for three hours, but he didn't mind. He'd done stakeouts much longer than this, sometimes days at a time. Hiding up in abandoned buildings in Gaza, pissing in bottles and eating energy bars, knowing that at any moment they could be discovered and fired upon. Sitting in the comfortable leather seats of the Range Rover in the relative safety of a Dubai Industrial Estate was heavenly compared to that.

But he felt he had waited enough and was itching to get moving. The guard hadn't moved for an hour, and Max guessed by the angle of his head that he was sleeping. There had been no movement in the street for two hours. Deciding it was safe enough to move, he reached into the sports bag in the passenger footwell and removed a balaclava. He pulled it onto his head and over his face, then pulled on a pair of latex gloves. Starting up the Range Rover and keeping the lights off, he rolled slowly toward the warehouse. He pulled up just short of the gate, then ensuring the interior light was off, and leaving the engine running, retrieved a handful of zip ties and a roll of duct tape from the sports bag, opened the door and climbed out. Without stopping, he moved swiftly toward the guard hut, yanked open the door, and rushed inside. He had his hand over the guard's mouth before he was fully awake and he pulled him to the ground and flipped him onto his stomach within seconds.

"Ismat," Max growled in Arabic. "Keep quiet."

The old man said nothing, his panicked breathing the only sign that he was aware of what was going on. Max zip-tied his hands together behind his back, then ripped off a piece of duct tape and, turning the man over, stuck it over his mouth. The old man's eyes darted around in panic, his thin chest pumping up and down.

Max fastened his ankles together, then sat back on his heels.

"I won't hurt you, *'amm,"* Max continued in Arabic.

The man blinked rapidly, his eyes showing he didn't believe Max.

"I promise, but I need your help. If you help me, everything will be okay, and I'll call the police to come and let you go. But if you don't...." Max left the threat hanging. "Do you understand me?"

This time, the man nodded.

"Is there anyone in the building?"

The man shook his head.

"Where are the keys?"

The man's eyes shifted toward a small cabinet on the wall. Max stood up and opened it. There was a bunch of keys on a hook. He took them and spread the four keys out.

"Which one is the front door key?" Max asked. He pointed to the first key, and the man shook his head. He did the same with the second, the man only nodding when he pointed at the third key of the bunch. "Good, *shukraan*. Is there an alarm?"

The man nodded and jerked his head toward the desk. Max stood again and moved over to the desk and looked back at the old man. The old man grunted and tried to say something with his eyes and his eyebrows.

Max looked down at the desktop. There was a leather-bound notebook beside the keypad. He held it up and the old man nodded. Opening it, Max saw each page had a date and then a series of numbers written beneath it: the alarm codes. He leafed through the book, noting the codes were changed every week. He shook his head. Changing the codes was a good idea only until you wrote them down in a book for anyone to find. Leafing through until he found the current week, he then tore the page from the book and stuffed it into his pocket. He then ran his eyes over the monitors, tracing the cables down to a hard drive beneath the desk. He pulled all the cables out and turned off the power before turning back to look at the old man on the floor.

"*Shukraan, 'amm*. Thank you, uncle. Now don't worry. The police will find you here soon."

———

36

Max backed the Range Rover up to the front door of the offices at the front of the warehouse and climbed out. Using the security guard's key, he opened the door and scanned the entrance for the alarm panel. A flashing red light gave it away, and he quickly removed the paper from his pocket and punched in the code. The light stopped flashing. So far, so good.

He went back outside and took a quick look up and down the street. Still silent.

From the rear of the Range Rover, he removed a jerry can and hauled it inside. Unscrewing the top, he then began moving through the offices, splashing petrol liberally over the desks and computers. The jerry can was soon empty, and he went back to the Range Rover and removed another. This time, he carried it through the offices and through a connecting door that led into the warehouse. It was pitch black inside, and he pulled out a penlight from his pocket and switched it on. The beam played across rows of stacked cardboard cartons, wooden pallets stacked with tinned food, and sacks of grain and rice.

Max hesitated for just a moment. It seemed a crime to waste so much food, but he reasoned it was for a higher purpose. This was the business of a man who dealt in a product that destroyed lives. Max quickly emptied the contents of the jerry can over the nearest row of cartons and sacks, then tossed the jerry can onto the floor. He moved back to the office door while retrieving a steel zippo from his pocket. Flicking it open, he lit a flame and tossed it toward the petrol soaked cartons. There was a whoosh and a rush of heat and blue flame.

Max quickly stepped back into the office and pulled out a second lighter. He moved to the front door before turning around and repeating the process with the second zippo. As the flames burst into life, he stepped back outside, closed the door, jumped into the Range Rover and pulled out of the carpark with a chirp of tires and a roar of the powerful V8 engine. At the end of the street, just before making the turn, a bright flash of light appeared in his mirrors as the fire burst through the windows of the offices.

Max grinned. Another successful night's work.

37

There was an irritating buzzing sound, and Liam groaned, pulling the duvet cover over his head. Bloody mosquitoes. The buzzing continued until he realise what he was hearing was his phone and not a blood-sucking insect.

He sat up quickly, groaned as the sudden rush of blood caused his temples to throb, then reached for the brightly glowing phone that was shifting across the top of the bedside table as it vibrated.

Without waiting to see who was calling, he pressed the phone to his ear. "Hello?"

His chest tightened as the caller spoke and he screwed up his face and clenched his fist. He fought to keep control of his emotions, still listening, nodding as if the caller was in the same room, and then ended the call with a simple, "Okay."

He slammed the phone down on the bed and roared, "For fuck's sake!" Grabbing the pillow from behind him, he buried his face in it, screaming with frustration. He dropped the pillow onto the bed and began punching it with rage before hurling it across the room. His initial rage temporarily spent, he sat staring into the darkness, his chest rising and falling rapidly as he panted. His heart pounded in his temples and a tremor ran down his arms and into his fingers. Nausea swept through him, bile rising in his throat, and he gulped down the mixture of stomach acid and expensive Irish whiskey.

Eventually, he slowed his breathing, took several deep breaths and swung his legs off the bed. He paused for a moment, unable to believe how bad things had become, then stood up and made his way unsteadily across the dark bedroom to the door. Wrenching it open, he shouted, "Barry! Get yourself in here!"

Ten minutes later, the two men were sitting at the dining table while a sleepy Joy brewed coffee in the kitchen.

Barry sat back in his chair, his arms crossed, staring at the tabletop while Liam tapped an irritated rhythm with his forefinger on the polished mahogany surface. They hadn't spoken for five minutes, both digesting the news that one of Liam's distribution centres had burnt to the ground. It was an enormous shock to both of them following so closely after the attack on the villa and the sinking of the 'High Seas'. In the history of their relationship, they had never experienced so many attacks in such a short time.

Joy placed a silver tray containing a samovar of coffee and two cups on the table between the two men. "I made the cookies you like, sir." She nodded at the plate of cookies on the tray. "Freshly baked last night," she added hesitantly as the two men failed to respond. She took a step back, looking from one to the other. "Will there be anything else, sir?" she asked Liam.

Liam grunted but didn't look up.

Barry raised a hand to get her attention and shook his head. "Go back to sleep, Joy. No point in you staying awake."

She nodded, still unsure, and with another glance at Liam, took another step back before wiping her hands on her apron.

Only when she had left the two men alone, did Liam look up. He blinked at the samovar in surprise, then looked toward the kitchen.

"I sent her back to bed," Barry explained, then reached forward and poured two cups of coffee. He slid one across the table to Liam, then sat back in his chair, holding the cup with both hands and watching the steam spiralling off the top.

Liam said nothing. His entire world had come tumbling down around him and for the first time in his life, he didn't know what to do.

He stared at the cup of coffee in his hand, then placed it back down on the table. Looking up, he said, "I have to go back."

Barry narrowed his eyes, but said nothing.

"I need to be on the ground. I have to be there. I can't fix this while hiding like a scared little boy here in Oman."

Barry was shaking his head, but Liam held up his hand. "You heard what Stavros said last night. Sharif. Pavel. You heard them all. There's no respect anymore. They're all sitting there waiting, like vultures circling a dying animal. They can't wait to move in." Liam shook his head, looking down at his untouched coffee again. "After all, I've done for the bastards." Looking up, he said, "and Hakim. He's not taking this seriously. He thinks I'm out of sight and therefore he has nothing to worry about. I want to go back and look him in the eyes. Show him he can't mess with me. And if that still doesn't work, I'm going to visit his wife and give her a photography lesson."

"No," Barry finally spoke.

"What?" Liam frowned.

"No. You stay here." Barry growled. "It's not safe for you to go back. Not yet. We don't know who we're dealing with or how many. We don't know if the police are looking for you, too. I mean, how much can you trust Hakim? It's too risky."

"Then what the fuck do you think I should do then, Barry? Sit here all day, drinking coffee and..." he gestured at the table, "eating fucking cookies with you?"

"I'll go."

"You?" Liam replied, both eyebrows raised at first, then he relaxed them and nodded slowly. "And what will you do?"

"What I do best."

Liam studied his friend for a long time, then nodded. "Okay."

D espite the warm breeze blowing across the road, the old man sitting on the back step of the ambulance had a blanket wrapped around his shoulders. He looked thin and frail, white stubble across sunken cheeks and upon seeing Colonel Hakim in his full police uniform, more than a little frightened.

A paramedic unfastened the blood pressure cuff from the man's upper arm and then, with a nod at Hakim, stepped away as he rolled it up and stowed it in the back of the ambulance.

Hakim glanced at his notebook, skimming the notes Major Omar had taken earlier, finding nothing of use. Apart from the old man, there were no witnesses, and the security cameras had been turned off. Hakim sighed and looked around. The fire was out but smoke and steam still rose from the burnt out hulk of the warehouse, the smell of smoke and chemicals hanging heavy in the air.

Hakim looked down at the glistening road surface, the emergency lights reflected in the wet surface while a stream of water trickled along the gutter. For the third morning in a row, Hakim had been roused from his bed to attend a crime scene. For the third time in a row, the crime scene involved Liam Mulroney.

Hakim turned back to look at the elderly security guard. He felt sorry for him. He probably thought he'd see out his remaining years with a quiet job and a steady income. After all, nothing really happened in such a safe city. He suppressed a snort, even though he'd only said it in his mind. It wasn't safe any longer, and the way things were going, neither was Hakim's job.

"So you didn't see his face at all?" Hakim knew the answer, but thought he should ask something, if only to feel like he was doing his job.

The old man shook his head without looking up.

"And you remember nothing noticeable about him? There must be something," Hakim prodded, a hint of frustration in his tone.

The man looked up and studied Hakim, his eyes running over his face and then his uniform. He then just shook his head and looked away.

Hakim ground his teeth together and once more looked down at the notes. A man in black… a balaclava covering his face… spoke Arabic… had kind eyes. Hakim shook his head in disbelief and once again looked over at the old man. He was about to say something to him, then thought better of it. It wouldn't help. He exhaled loudly, slipped Omar's notebook into his pocket, and turned away.

Emergency vehicles and personnel filled the street. Fire crew making the site safe and stowing their equipment, the paramedics tending to the old man, and his own men standing around with nothing to do. He spotted Omar talking to a firefighter, and he walked over. Omar noticed him approaching, and he nodded at the firefighter, shook his hand, and walked toward Hakim.

"Well?" Hakim asked.

"They found the remains of a jerry can in the building, so they believe it's arson, sir."

"Huh," Hakim scoffed. He removed Omar's notebook from his pocket and handed it over. "The tied up security guard would have been a major hint."

"I just wanted confirmation, sir," Omar replied defensively, taking the notebook from Hakim. "I have to be thorough."

Hakim exhaled loudly. He shouldn't take his frustration out on the Major. He was doing his job and doing it well. Hakim smiled. "Yes, I know, Omar." He reached out and placed a hand on Omar's shoulder. "Good work."

"There's something else you should know, sir."

"What's that, Omar?"

"Atlas Regional Trading FZCO is also owned by Liam Mulroney. The same man who owns the 'High Seas', and the villa on The Palm."

Hakim nodded. He knew that, too. He'd had an earful from Liam just a short time ago. But he wasn't about to let his men know. "Is that right?" was all he could think of to say.

"Sir... this is not just a coincidence."

"No. It doesn't seem like it."

"What do you want me to do, sir?"

Hakim stared at the burnt out building while he thought. To be honest, he didn't know what to do. They had no leads, and he had the added stress of Liam's blackmail material hanging over his head. He had to get a break. Surely whoever was carrying out these attacks would slip up soon, and when that happened, Liam and his men had to be ready.

Turning back to Omar, he said, "We have to assume it's going to happen again and we have to put a stop to it as soon as possible. Let's put together a list of properties owned by Liam Mulroney and we'll step up patrols. Maybe we can catch these people in the act next time?"

"Yes, sir," Omar replied. He stood looking down at his feet, and Hakim could sense he wanted to say something.

"Is there something else?"

Omar swallowed and looked up. "Sir, are you not telling me something?"

Hakim frowned. "What do you mean?"

"It's... it's just that, the men we rounded up the other night. They all have a certain reputation..." he trailed off.

"Come on. Say what you mean."

"Well, is there more to Liam Mulroney than it looks like?" Omar took a breath. "There was a shootout at his home, now these attacks," Omar gestured at the warehouse. "And you have me rounding up men who are widely rumoured to be involved in the local drug trade. Is this a turf war?"

Hakim thought carefully about how to reply. Omar was a loyal and trusted man. They had worked together for a long time and respected each other. Hakim didn't want to lose that respect but also could never let him know about the money he'd been taking from Liam Mulroney for years or about the blackmail material. He had to tread carefully. "As far as we know, Liam Mulroney is a legitimate business-man. There has been no evidence to the contrary. But...." He took a deep breath. This is where he had to be careful. "There have been rumours, and after the shootout the other night, there is possibly some truth behind them. I don't know. We just have to do our job and see what turns up."

"So that's why you had me round up Stavros Nikolaidas and the others?" Omar tilted his head to one side, frowning deeply.

"Yes. I asked myself if the rumours were true and someone wanted to take over Liam's business, who would it be? But I was wrong. Those men knew nothing."

Omar didn't appear convinced, but deferred to his boss.

"So maybe we have to look further afield. Perhaps he's upset someone in one of the countries he does business in. But only he'll know that."

"Have you spoken to him?" Omar asked.

"Briefly, on the phone." Hakim turned away and once more looked at the smoldering building. "He's out of the country right now," he continued. "As soon as he's back, we'll have a proper conversation."

"Okay, sir."

Hakim hoped he'd said enough to allay Omar's doubts, but it wouldn't last for long. Omar was a clever policeman with good instincts. He wouldn't be able to pull the wool over his eyes for long. There was now a constant pressure in Hakim's chest that had been growing since the shootout. He had to find a solution soon.

39

B arry eased the big Nissan Patrol off the road and onto the sandy track that led deep into the Hajar Mountains. The sun had already dropped behind the mountains and the light had dimmed considerably. Once away from the road, Barry flicked on the powerful spotlights, lighting up the dry *wadi* ahead. Drifts of sand covered the stony ground and Barry slowed to a stop, put the gearbox in neutral and engaged low range. Pressing his foot down on the accelerator, the powerful 4.8 litre engine roared, and he rolled forward, the sudden noise and movement shattering the early evening silence. In the distance, at the far reaches of the spotlight beam, two points of light briefly shone, before hurrying out of sight, a wolf or perhaps a caracal out on its evening hunt.

Barry glanced at the digital clock on the dashboard. He had plenty of time and planned to enjoy his moment of solitude for as long as he could. The last few days had been incredibly stressful, and the days ahead promised to be equally so. So he would enjoy the drive through the mountains and back across the border into Dubai while he could.

He had left the G-Wagen behind with Liam. He wanted something more generic, less likely to stand out, and besides, he wasn't sure if the police were on the lookout for Liam's vehicles. Instead, he had picked up the Nissan from a local car dealer, the big white SUV very common on the roads of the Middle East and very handy off-road, too. It was unlikely to be noticed and once across the border, he'd swap out the plates for a Dubai registration, further making the car invisible.

He'd spent the morning making calls, bringing in some hired muscle from some of the other countries in which they did business. Hard men who weren't afraid to get their hands dirty. Two men from Egypt, ex *El-Sa'Ka* Special Forces, and Khalid from Saudi Arabia, an ex-paratrooper who promised to bring a couple of men with him and some weapons. The Egyptians were flying in that night, but the Saudis would take longer to arrive. Because of the weapons, they couldn't fly and instead were driving across the border in the *Rub' al Khali*, the empty quarter, one of the largest sand deserts in the world. It would be a day or so before they would reach Muscat.

Liam had insisted he didn't need protection, but Barry wasn't comfortable leaving him alone. Barry had made it his life's mission to look after Liam, so it was better to be safe than sorry. They had no idea who they were dealing with, but whoever it was had taken out Liam's entire Dubai team with ease. Barry felt much more comfortable leaving him behind with some skilled armed men to watch over him.

He'd rested once the calls were done, trying to catch up on sleep, but it had proved elusive. In the end, he sat with Liam, drinking coffee and trying to work out what their attacker might do. They had gone through a list of proper- ties in Dubai, guessing which one would be hit next.

Ignoring the rental apartments and two empty villas, they decided the focus would be on the commercial properties. There were three of them, so it would still be down to luck whether he would catch the attackers in the act. In fact, Barry would need a lot of luck. With their team in Dubai decimated, he had no manpower to call on. It was down to him.

He settled back in his seat and pushed the thoughts into the back of his mind. That was for tomorrow. For now, he would enjoy the desert drive.

40

L ike Barry, Max too had spent the day recharging his batteries. He had slept a deep dreamless sleep, late into the morning, the blackout drapes of the hotel room doing a good job of keeping the light out of the room.

Just after eleven, he got up, feeling refreshed and renewed. Pulling back the drapes, he stretched and yawned as the light came flooding in. Turning back, he noticed a note slipped under the door to the connecting room.

"Didn't want to wake you. I'll be back this evening. Call me if you need me. Azar."

Max grinned. Azar didn't enjoy being left out.

Max spent the next three quarters of an hour exercising in his room. Sun salutations followed by rounds of press-ups and bodyweight squats until his body glistened with sweat and his lungs heaved with the effort.

He showered and changed, then sat on the bed, closed his eyes, and spent half an hour focusing on his breathing and meditating until his mind settled and his entire being glowed with well-being. The past few days had taken a toll on him, both physically and mentally. This wasn't a new experience; during his days as a soldier, he had faced similar strains that left lasting scars on his mental state and exhausted him physically.

While his colleagues turned to stimulants—amphetamines, Captagon, even cocaine—to keep going, Max had tried them once or twice but found them unsatisfying. The drugs left him feeling hollow, the energy artificial, and they did nothing to ease the nightmares that haunted his nights. It was only when he joined Georges, running security for the guru Atman, that he discovered a semblance of peace. The techniques Atman had taught him—exercises, pranayama, and meditation—gradually eased his PTSD, allowing him to sleep through the night and diminishing the guilt that had gnawed at him for so long.

Now, after his exercise and meditation, he felt more alive than he ever had under the influence of artificial stimulants. He was calm, at peace, yet brimming with energy.

While enjoying a room service lunch of steak and eggs, washed down with strong black coffee, Max revisited the list of properties.

Several options were immediately discounted, particularly the apartments in residential buildings. He wanted to minimize collateral damage, and those locations posed too many risks. Gaining access would be challenging, they were tenanted, and the potential for fire to spread to neighboring properties was too high. This cut the list down significantly. The highest-value targets were already gone—the yacht, the warehouse, and, of course, the villa on The Palm, where it had all begun. Liam Mulroney had to be feeling the impact by now, but Max still had no clue where the man was hiding. He needed to do more to flush him out and provoke some sort of reaction.

Max whittled the list down to two targets. Once he finished his lunch, he headed down to the basement to retrieve the Range Rover.

It was another forty minutes along the traffic snarled Sheikh Zayed Road before Max turned once again into the Jebel Ali Free Zone, or JAFZA. So named because of their tax free status, the free zones were popular with foreign-owned businesses.

Just twelve hours earlier, Max had stood in the darkness, successfully setting fire to the warehouse of Atlas Regional Trading. He resisted the urge to check on the damage; the less he was seen in the area, the better. Instead, he focused on identifying a new target. Liam Mulroney owned two more warehouses: the empty one from which he had rescued the girls almost a week ago and another in the Free Zone. While Max had scouted it using Google Street View, he knew nothing compared to visiting the location in person. There were details that could only be observed on-site, and the photos on Google could be outdated, taken years before.

Max checked the map on his phone before slowing down and turning off the dual carriageway onto a narrower two-lane road lined with industrial buildings. The sides of the road were filled with car and truck parking, interspersed with patches of sand and scrub. Here and there, acacia trees and palms struggled to thrive amidst the sand and concrete, their dusty green contrasting with the surroundings. He took another turn past a site filled with rows of parked yellow construction equipment, including dump trucks and cranes, then passed several nondescript warehouses clad in beige aluminum, their lower levels cluttered with air conditioning units and fan outlets. After another two hundred meters, he turned again, double-checked the map, and cruised slowly along a narrower, sand-strewn road. It felt as though he had left the glitz and glamour of Dubai behind, entering a poorer, less developed area. Vacant patches of land were littered with construction waste and plastic bags, while abandoned warehouses crumbled slowly into the desert. Rows of empty tractor-trailers lined the sandy roadside, occasionally punctuated by a warehouse or factory that showed signs of life, with battered pickup trucks and Japanese cars gathering sand as their owners worked inside. This was a far cry from the Dubai most visitors experienced.

Anticipating the sight of Liam Mulroney's warehouse ahead on the right, Max reduced his speed and scanned the surroundings for anything he could use to his advantage. The warehouse came into view, smaller than the one he had burned the previous night, but from the looks of the parking lot, it was still in use. Several cars lined the front of the building, and a medium-sized truck was backed into the loading bay. Through the open loading bay doors, he glimpsed a forklift moving around and several workers busy with their tasks. He rolled past as slowly as possible to avoid drawing suspicion, taking note of the chain-link fence topped with barbed wire and the steel gate on rollers. On his first pass, he didn't spot any cameras but knew he would need to drive by again to be sure.

As he neared the end of the road, where it turned left, he prepared to make a U-turn when a vehicle came around the corner, causing his heart to race and his breath to catch in his throat. A white SUV with green hood and stripes—the unmistakable markings of the Dubai Police—rolled toward him in the opposite lane. Max quickly turned his face away, pretending to look out the passenger side window as it

passed. Once it was behind him, he glanced up into the
rear-view mirror, anxiously watching for the flash of brake
lights or the lights on the roof-mounted light bar—anything
that would indicate they had spotted him. He tensed as the
brake lights flashed on, the Ford Explorer turning left. Max
took the corner at the end of the street and looked over his
shoulder, ready to mash the accelerator and make his
escape, but the police vehicle instead turned into the car
parking of Liam Mulroney's warehouse. Max frowned. Was
it just a coincidence? He drove on for two hundred metres,
then pulled off the road into the sandy verge and pulled to a
stop. His eyes on the rear-view mirror, he sat and thought
about what he'd just seen.

They didn't seem to be looking for the Range Rover,
which was a relief, but why were they there?

He sat for a minute then sticking the vehicle in drive,
swung a u-turn and headed back the way he had come.
Rounding the corner, he spotted the police SUV still in the
carpark, the driver and his companion standing outside the
vehicle. He drove past, watching them from the side of his
eyes, not looking directly. They were both facing away from
the road, both looking at the building while one spoke into
a handheld radio.

Max chewed his lip. It was to be expected, he reasoned.
Attacks on three of Liam's properties were bound to bring
an increased police presence, but for how long? And would
they be there the whole time? Would they be at all his
properties?

Max banged the steering wheel and shook his head. Too
many unknowns.

An hour later, having checked the other warehouse on
his list and finding another police vehicle outside, Max
came to a decision. He would take the night off and hold off

any more attacks for a night or two. Let the attention die down. Lull them into a false sense of safety. There was only so long the police would devote these kind of resources to guarding private properties, no matter what leverage Liam had over them.

41

L iam stopped by the large green bush covered in white star-shaped flowers and took a deep breath, inhaling the sweet intense fragrance of Arabian Jasmine. He nodded with satisfaction and turned to smile at his gardener. "Beautiful. It's growing well, Abdullah."

"Thank you, sir."

Liam turned around, his gaze encompassing the expanse of his garden, the lush green lawns, the flowerbeds filled with marigolds, geraniums, the brightly coloured bougainvillea covering the boundary walls. He'd forgotten how much he enjoyed coming here. It was a peaceful little oasis in the stressful desert of his life. He only wished he was here under better circumstances. Pushing away the irritation that was threatening to make its presence known again, he walked over to the row of hibiscus and frowned. "What's happened here?" he asked, pointing at the yellowing and wilted leaves.

"Mealybugs, sir," Abdullah replied, squatting down and pointing at the white cotton like clusters on the stems.

"How do we get rid of them?"

"There's an oil spray I can use. Neem."

Again the irritation rose its head. "So, what are you waiting for?"

Abdullah ducked his head submissively. "Yes, sir. Sorry, sir."

Liam regained control, reaching out a hand and placing it on the gardener's arm. "Let me know if there is anything else you need." He smiled. "The garden is looking very good."

Abdullah's face coloured slightly as his smile returned.

"Do we have enough water?" Liam asked, conscious that just on the other side of the wall was a barren, sandy, stony landscape.

"Yes, *alhamdulillah*. By God's grace. A lot of water."

"Good." Liam looked around the garden again, then clapped Abdullah on the shoulder. "Keep up the good work."

Liam walked away, continuing his walk around the garden, more to keep himself occupied than anything else. The day had passed slowly, with no news from Barry apart from a text that simply said '*arrived.*'

Liam crossed the lawn, passing the main gate where one of the new men sat on a stool in the shade of a Flame Tree. He was unarmed; the weapons hopefully arriving later that night with the Saudis. He stood as Liam approached and nodded a respectful greeting.

"All okay? Hassan, isn't it?"

"Yes sir. All quiet, sir." The man smiled, flashing brilliant white teeth in a deeply lined and tanned face.

Liam nodded. "What time does your shift end?"

The man turned his wrist and glanced at the steel wristwatch on his wrist. "Another hour, sir. Then Youssef will relieve me."

"Okay. Let me know if there's anything you need. The other men should arrive later tonight, and then I'll shorten the shifts."

"Thank you, sir."

Liam smiled and nodded, then continued on his way. He hated having nothing to do, but couldn't focus on legitimate work while someone was out there trying to destroy him. He should be filing insurance claims, arranging the salvage of his boat, or dealing with angry customers who wouldn't get the foodstuffs they had paid for. Worse still were the drug clients who had paid in advance for shipments that wouldn't arrive. His drug business relied on trust—no contracts or legal options to fall back on. Once trust was lost, it was nearly impossible to regain. But Liam couldn't bring himself to care. His emotions were all over the place. Anger domi-nated most of the time, but now and then, grief would surface, especially when something reminded him of his murdered brother.

Liam stopped beside the swimming pool and stared at the turquoise blue surface, the ripples catching the rays of the setting sun.

It had been a long time since both of them had been in Muscat together. Back then, things were better between them. They'd shared a few cold beers by the pool, remi-niscing about their childhood in Ireland. But over the years, their relationship had soured. Caim spent more time drinking and chasing women, while Liam focused on running the business, hoping it was just a phase. He started sidelining Caim, keeping him out of decisions. Caim grew sullen and resentful. Liam tried to help by giving him his own businesses to run, but they kept failing, and Caim got into more trouble with the Dubai authorities—fighting and getting arrested for being drunk and disorderly. Eventually, Liam shut him out completely. They couldn't spend time together without arguing. Liam sighed. If only he'd handled things differently, Caim might still be around, and his business wouldn't be under attack.

42

"Your salmon, sir."

Hakim smiled up at the young waiter. "Thank you."

The waiter returned his smile, then turned to Latifah and respectfully bowed his head before backing away and leaving them alone.

Latifah's eyes sparkled in the candlelight and she reached across the table and touched Hakim's hand.

"Thank you, *habibi*."

Hakim turned his hand over, taking hers in his, and gave it a squeeze. "I'm sorry, *habibti*, this is long overdue."

Latifah took a shy glance around the restaurant, then blew him a kiss and giggled.

Hakim gazed back at the love of his life, warmth spreading through him. A lock of chestnut hair slipped from the black silk *shayla* framing her face, highlighting her hazel eyes—unusual for an Emirati woman—and her high cheek-bones. She was just as beautiful as the day he first saw her on the campus of Zayed University. She had taken his breath away then, and even now, with the soft lines of motherhood and the passage of time, she remained as stunning as ever.

An image of the photos in his drawer flashed briefly in his mind, and he swallowed hard, loosening his grip on her hand. How could he have been so foolish? The warmth in their relationship had faded over the years, but it wasn't her fault. The girls consumed all her time, and his work kept him out late, leaving him tired and irritable when he was home. It had strained their marriage, and instead of addressing the issues, he had taken the easy way out. He sought comfort in the arms of Western women, convincing himself it was harmless—just a physical release. But deep down, he knew it was wrong, long before that *ibn al-haram*, that bastard Liam Mulroney, began blackmailing him.

"Is there something wrong, *habibi*?"

"What?" Hakim looked up in surprise, not realizing he had drifted off.

"Your face changed."

"No no, I'm sorry." He smiled, pushing his thoughts back into the recesses of his mind. "I just remembered something at work. But tonight there's no work. Just us."

Latifah cocked her head to the side and smiled.

"How's your pasta?" Hakim nodded toward her plate.

"I don't know yet. I'll try it now."

Hakim grinned and picked up his cutlery. "We should do this more often. Now the girls are older." He sliced a portion of salmon and speared it with his fork. "The new babysitter seems okay?"

"Yes," Latifah replied as she twirled her fettuccine on her fork and popped it into her mouth. "Mmm," she exclaimed. "Delicious."

Hakim grinned and tasted his salmon. It, too, was delicious, grilled to perfection.

"How did you find her?" he asked once he had swallowed.

"Noor recommended her. You remember Noor?"

Hakim shook his head. The only thing he remembered was work.

"She's the mother of Laila, Sariah's friend from school."

Hakim grunted as if he knew who she was and stuffed another mouthful of salmon in his mouth. His mind wandered off again, only half listening to the conversation.

He had to find a solution. He couldn't spend the rest of his life worrying about the photos.

"Is this place expensive?"

"Sorry?"

"It looks expensive, Hakim *habibi*. Can we afford it?"

Hakim put down his knife and held his finger to his lips. "Don't ask questions like that. This is my treat for the woman I love. The mother of my two beautiful girls. Nothing is too expensive."

Latifah beamed, her eyes becoming moist. "I love you, Hakim."

"I love you too, *habibti*." And he meant it—he truly did. He loved her with all his heart, but that love was clouded by guilt and a deep sense of failure.

43

Max waited two more days before making his next move. He had considered acting sooner, but after several reconnaissance runs in the Range Rover, he realized the police were still keeping a close watch on Liam's properties. On the third day, during one of his daytime drive-bys, he noticed the police presence had thinned out. Later in the day, the building was still being ignored. He even parked nearby for an hour, watching, but apart from the warehouse staff, no one paid it any attention. So he decided to hit the building in the early hours of the morning.

He would stick to setting it on fire. It was easy and had worked before. No sense in re-inventing the wheel.

He lay now on top of his hotel room bed, fully clothed, trying to get some sleep before heading out.

Max glanced at the digital clock on the bedside table— still a couple of hours before he should leave. Everything was ready. The jerry cans of petrol, paid for in cash, were stashed in the trunk of the Range Rover. He'd even swapped out the number plates in a supermarket parking lot, just in case the vehicle had been spotted during the last fire. He was dressed all in black, ready to go. There was nothing left to do but wait and unless he slept, the time would drag.

Closing his eyes, he exhaled slowly before taking a long inward breath, holding it, then exhaling again. He continued the process, in for four counts, hold for seven counts, then exhaled for eight counts. Starting at his feet, he consciously relaxed each body part, working his way up his body. It was a technique that had served him well before, when he'd been serving, and sleep was a valuable commodity.

An internal alarm woke him. He opened his eyes and stared into the darkness of the room. Turning his head, he noted the time. Two am. Perfect. The sleep technique definitely worked. He remembered getting as far as relaxing his shoulders, but not any further. Sitting up, he stretched, mentally checking for any tension or unease. He felt refreshed and ready to go.

By 2:30 a.m., Max was cruising slowly through the empty streets of the Jebel Ali Free Zone. The place was completely still—no one around, nothing moving. With the windows rolled down, he paused a little longer at each intersection, listening and checking his mirrors. As far as he could tell, he was alone.

He turned onto the street where Liam's warehouse was located and eased off the gas. The place looked even more rundown at night. The streetlights cast a dull, washed-out glow, making everything appear in faded shades of beige and grey.

Max scanned the roadside and surrounding buildings, looking for anything unusual. A few more empty tractor-trailers were lined up along the street, but the parking lots of the nearby buildings were deserted. A white Nissan Patrol parked in the middle of the line caught his eye. Slowing down as he passed, he noticed it was empty, its dusty exterior suggesting it had been sitting there for a while. He must have overlooked it earlier in the day.

He drove past Liam's warehouse, dark and locked for the night. There were no guards, and no security cameras—a much easier target, but he would still have to be careful. He continued down the road, took a turn around the block, and made a u-turn to come back the other way.

Nothing seemed out of place. No signs of a threat, and no sign of the police.

Max checked his mirrors one last time, then brought the car to a stop just before the entrance to the warehouse. He sat for a moment, listening, his eyes constantly scanning the surroundings. When he was certain he was alone, he turned into the warehouse parking lot, swung the vehicle in a half-circle, then backed up to the front door of the office and climbed out.

44

B arry was exhausted and frustrated. After sneaking back into Dubai, he headed straight for a cheap guesthouse in Bur Dubai—a place that took cash and didn't ask too many questions about ID. He could've stayed in one of Liam's empty apartments, but he didn't want to risk anyone knowing he was there. He wasn't sure where things stood with the police. Liam claimed to trust Colonel Hakim, but Barry preferred to play it safe. There had been a shootout on the Palm resulting in the deaths of seven men, followed by a fire. There were bound to be repercussions no matter how much Liam was blackmailing the Colonel. Hakim was just one cop, and there were plenty of others Liam didn't control.

At the guesthouse, Barry managed to grab a couple of hours of sleep before hitting the streets to check in with his informants. He hoped that seeing him in person would make them more willing to share information than they had been over the phone, but it didn't help at all. No one knew anything. What frustrated him even more was that he believed them; they were dealing with a phantom—a ghost.

But Barry wasn't ready to throw in the towel. He had promised long ago to keep Liam safe, and he was a man of his word. Eventually, whoever was targeting Liam would slip up, and when that happened, Barry would be ready to act.

He spent his nights parked outside Liam's properties, waiting for another attack. He couldn't monitor them all, so he focused on the most likely targets—the ones he would hit if he were the attacker. At first, the police helped by making regular visits to the properties, and Barry did his best to stay out of sight. But it wasn't long before their patrols grew less frequent.

Barry reported this to Liam, who suggested he confront Hakim and threaten him. But Barry preferred to keep a low profile for now.

He yawned and checked his watch. When this was all over, he was going to sleep for a week. Sighing loudly, he checked to make sure the interior light of the Nissan was off before opening the door and climbing out. His bladder was bursting, and after three hours of sitting in the car, he needed to get his legs moving again.

He peeled his shirt away from his back and shook his legs out while looking up and down the empty street. It had been that way for the last three hours. No sign of a police patrol or anyone else. He walked around the Patrol and into the darkness behind the row of tractor-trailers. Stopping, he raised his arms above his head, stretching his back and feeling the pops and clicks as his spine lengthened. Then he unzipped his jeans, leaned against one of the trailers, and, with a satisfied sigh, relieved himself on the truck tires.

Barry was just finishing up, shaking off every last drop, when he heard the low rumble of a powerful engine. He zipped himself up and stayed put, hidden in the shadows, as a vehicle turned into the street, its headlights sweeping over the buildings. Pressing himself against the trailer, deep in shadow, he watched as the vehicle approached. It slowed as it passed and then carried on past the warehouse toward the corner.

Barry ducked down and peered under the trailer. It was a black Range Rover Sport, just like Liam had before it was stolen. Was it the attackers? His hand went for the Glock in his waistband, but he remembered he had left it in the Nissan even as he read the number plate. No, it wasn't the same vehicle. The registration was different. He watched it turn the corner and heard it drive away before allowing himself to relax. Probably nothing.

He stood and made his way back to the Nissan and climbed in. He would wait another hour and if no-one came, he would take a round of the other properties. Perhaps he had chosen the wrong one tonight.

He settled back in his seat, reclined just enough so his eye line was level with the door, and attempted to rub the tiredness from his eyes.

When he dropped his hands onto his lap, he noticed the glow of approaching headlights.

Stiffening, he lowered himself a fraction more and watched as the Range Rover returned from the opposite direction, the headlights blinding him. He closed one eye to keep half of his night vision and watched the vehicle pull to a stop in the middle of the road, facing him. Barry held his breath, every muscle in his body tensed. Had he been spotted?

After a long moment, the Range Rover turned into the warehouse parking lot, and Barry exhaled. He watched it turn a half circle and back up to the door. He reached beneath the seat with his right hand for his Glock and gripped the door handle with his left.

"I've got you now, you feckin gobshite!"

45

The Range Rover purred softly as Max crouched beside the door, shielded by the open tailgate. He worked at the locks with his pick, and within thirty seconds, he heard the satisfying click. Twisting the handle, he swung the door open.

Moving swiftly, Max stood up, grabbed two jerry cans from the back of the Range Rover, and stepped inside. This building was less secure than the previous warehouse he had torched—there was no security guard, no cameras, and so far, no sign of an alarm. Still, he didn't want to take any chances, so he had to move quickly. He dropped one jerry can at his feet, twisted the top off the other, and began splashing petrol across the office furniture. Once it was empty, he tossed it aside and went back for the other can.

There was a door leading into the warehouse, and he opened it, carrying the jerry can with him. A small amount of light filtered through skylights set high in the ceiling, just enough for Max to see a parked forklift and a row of cardboard cartons stacked on wooden pallets. Other than that, the warehouse was mostly empty. He removed the cap from the jerry can and splashed petrol generously over the fork-lift and then the row of cartons.

Once again, he discarded the empty jerry can, tossing it onto the concrete floor. He turned his wrist to check his watch. He had been inside for three minutes—too long.

He reached into his pocket for the zippo and flicked it open.

It failed to light.

Max tried again, but once more, the Zippo failed to spark. He took a deep breath, fighting back his frustration. He needed to stay calm; the lighter had to work. He had tested it in his hotel room. He took one more breath, then tried again.

Nothing.

Grimacing, he dropped it into his pocket, and thought fast. How else could he ignite the fuel?

Maybe there was a lighter in one of the office drawers? Someone had to be a smoker, the rabid anti-smoking rules of the West not having reached the Middle East. He turned and hurried for the door, and reentered the office. There was more light in the office, courtesy of the street lamp shining through the window, and he quickly scanned the desks for an ashtray. He didn't see one. He could feel the tension increasing in his body and he consciously willed himself to remain calm. He had been in worse situations before. At least he wasn't being shot at.

The cigarette lighter in the Range Rover.

That would work. He turned away from the office and hurried to the front door. As he stepped outside, everything went black.

46

M ajor Omar al-Farsi paused behind the large window and studied the man chained to the desk in the interview room.

The man had no identification and hadn't uttered a word since his men brought him in. Omar had learned over the years to assess people by their appearances, but this man made him uneasy. He appeared to be in his late twenties or early thirties, with a buzz-cut that emphasized his lean face. His beard wasn't neatly trimmed like that of most Emirati men, but it also wasn't long and unkempt, like many devout Muslims. He didn't have the usual discoloration on his forehead from prayer, either. His features suggested he was from the region, and his tanned skin was evidence of considerable time spent outdoors.

What troubled Omar was the man's complete lack of fear. He sat calmly, almost in a meditative state, staring directly at the two-way mirror as if he could see Omar behind it. He had maintained this stillness for over two hours, not responding to the constables' questions or even speaking to the medic who had treated the cut on the back of his head.

Omar flicked open the manila folder and glanced at the single sheet inside. It provided little information, just the location where he was apprehended and a list of the items found in his pockets. Sighing, he noted the time on his watch and then entered the room.

"The time is six am, Major Omar al-Farsi conducting the interview," he announced for the benefit of the camera and voice recorder as he entered the room. He dropped the file onto the desktop, pulled out a chair, and sat down.

The man opposite him looked back at him without expression.

"Hal tatakallam al-'arabiyyah?"

The man didn't respond, not even a blink.

Omar tried again, switching to English. "Do you speak English?"

Again, no response. Omar clenched his jaw. This would not be easy. Not the way he wanted to start his day.

Running out of languages, he switched back to Arabic. "Would you like something to drink, water, coffee?" Over the years, Omar had learned it was always more productive to make the prisoner believe he was on their side, but the man stared back without a single change in his expression, as if he hadn't heard a thing.

Omar took a deep breath, opened the file and made a show of studying the contents, even though he had already committed it to memory.

"You were caught attempting to set fire to a property in the Jebel Ali Free Zone," Omar began, raising an eyebrow as he stared at the man. "Caught in the act." He looked down at the file again, unable to match the man's steady gaze. "According to this report, a search revealed the following items in your possession: a lock picking set and a Zippo lighter. The property had been doused in petrol, and two empty jerry cans were found on the premises." He looked up again, adopting a stern expression. "The registration number of the Range Rover you were driving actually belongs to a white Toyota Corolla, which indicates the vehicle is stolen." He paused for effect. "It won't take us long to find the real owner."

Once again, the man remained silent, and Omar felt frustration rising within him. He closed the file and leaned back in his chair, crossing his arms over his chest.

Frowning deeply to emphasize the gravity of the situation, he said, "You're in a great deal of trouble. You will be locked away for a long time." He sighed dramatically, leaned forward, and spread his hands on the desk. "Talk to me. Allow me to help you. Share your story. Maybe we can make things go a little better for you?"

The man continued to stare back at him, showing no sign of discomfort or tension. Just as Omar was about to stand up, he heard the man speak for the first time.

"I will only speak to Colonel Hakim Al-Hamadi."

47

L iam Mulroney could hardly contain his excitement. After a frustrating three days with no news, no progress, things had finally turned in his favour.

"Give me half an hour." He could feel the excitement coursing through his body and a wide grin spread across his face. "I'll make sure he's ours and ours alone. Well done, Barry. I'll call you back soon."

Liam ended the call and punched the air in delight. "I've got you now, you motherfucker!" he exclaimed to the empty bedroom. He stood up, crossed the bedroom and opened the blackout drapes, allowing the early morning sun to flood in. He looked out at the garden, the blooms of the hibiscus spreading their petals for the sun, the doves foraging in the long shadows of the lawn, a family of mynahs flitting past the window. It was going to be a good day.

He rolled his shoulders back and moved his head from side to side, stretching his neck, then bounced up and down on his toes. He shadow boxed his reflection, still grinning, then announced to no-one in particular, "I'm back."

Turning back to the bed, he picked up the phone and dialled.

It rang for longer than he wanted, before a familiar voice muttered, *"Na'am?"*

"Is that the way you answer the phone to a friend, Hakim? Not very polite."

He heard Hakim clear his throat and then say, "Good morning."

"That's better, Hakim. A very good morning to you too. Now I've just had some good news."

"Okay," Hakim replied, a note of hesitancy in his voice.

"Yes, and now it's time for you to do the right thing."

"And what is that?"

"You have a man in custody. A man you caught on my property. I want him released to me."

There was a lengthy pause and then Hakim replied, "I can't do that."

Liam's grin slipped a little. "Yes, you can."

"There are procedures. The man was caught in the act. Attempting to set fire to a property."

"My property, Hakim, my property!" Liam growled.

"I know that, and enquiries are ongoing to see if he was involved in the previous arson attack. But he's in our custody and there is a process. You've got what you wanted."

Liam gripped the phone and injected as much venom into his tone as he could. "What I want, Hakim, is for that man to be released to me. I will deal with him. I'm not interested in your... process. I have a process of my own and I intend to carry it out."

Hakim said nothing.

"Did you hear me?"

"I heard you," came the reluctant reply.

"Call me when he's about to be released and I'll have my man pick him up." Liam ended the call before Hakim could object and stared down at the phone in his hand. Hakim would release him. Of that, he was sure. He smiled to himself. He couldn't wait to get his hands on the man.

48

"Nothing at all?"

"Nothing, sir. He only insisted he speak to you."

Hakim frowned and studied the man on the other side of the two-way mirror. The man who stared straight back at him. It was quite disconcerting.

"So we know nothing about him at all?"

"Nothing sir. No identification, nothing in his possession to give us any clues. The car we think is stolen..."

"It's Liam Mulroney's," Hakim interrupted.

Omar nodded. "I thought so, sir, but we're still checking the VIN."

Hakim sniffed, his mind racing. What was he supposed to do? Liam's barked instructions echoed around inside his head, but it wasn't that easy. He'd have to think of an excellent reason to release the man and still keep the respect of his men. He took a deep breath and then exhaled loudly. "Okay. I'd better hear what he has to say."

Omar nodded and stepped back, allowing Hakim easy access to the door. Hakim paused with his hand on the door handle, took another deep breath, and then stepped inside. He closed the door behind him and stood looking at the man who had requested him by name. There was no recognition in the man's eyes, so how did he know him?

Hakim checked his watch and then announced to the recording equipment, "Seven thirty a.m. Interview conducted by Colonel Hakim Al-Hamadi."

"I suggest you turn that off." The man spoke in Arabic, and Hakim automatically searched his memory, trying to place the accent. Palestinian perhaps, but slightly different. Something wasn't right, but he couldn't place what it was. Hakim frowned. "It's not your place to make suggestions," he replied.

The corner of the man's mouth twitched in a slight smile. "You will not want what I'm about to share to be common knowledge."

Hakim stood over the man, thinking, then shrugged. He turned and nodded toward the two-way mirror. The man at the table turned his head to look up at the camera and when the light went off, he nodded. "Good. Please sit down."

Hakim blinked in surprise, a ball of anger igniting in his stomach. Who did this man think he was? He hesitated, then pulled out the chair and sat down.

"Who are you?" he asked.

The man smiled. "That's not important."

"Not important?" Hakim protested indignantly. "You've been caught performing a criminal act. I'm pretty sure you're also responsible for several others. You're facing a lengthy prison time. I think it's about time you cooperate."

The man leaned forward and raised his unchained hand to cover his mouth. When he spoke, it was in a low volume, so Hakim had to strain to hear.

"I don't know if your colleagues can lip read, so for your sake, I'm covering my mouth."

"For my sake?"

The man nodded and beckoned Hakim closer. Hakim, still frowning deeply, hesitated, but then acquiesced, leaning forward over the table. The man came closer, uncomfortably closer, their heads almost touching. "I know you've been taking money from Liam Mulroney."

The words sent a shiver of horror down Hakim's spine. He opened his mouth, but then closed it again.

"I also know Liam Mulroney is blackmailing you." The man sat back in his chair and smiled at Hakim.

Hakim swallowed and involuntarily looked up at the camera to make sure it was still turned off. His thoughts raced at a hundred miles an hour as he struggled to register what he'd just been told. Who was this man and how did he know? Was he bluffing?

Gathering some composure, Hakim replied, "I don't know what you're talking about."

The man smiled again. He leaned forward, again shielding his mouth from view, "I have proof. Bank records, photos. I know everything."

Hakim could feel his world collapsing. If this man knew, then how many others did too?

The man spoke again, so softly that Hakim thought he had misheard him.

"What did you say?" he asked.

"I said, I can help you."

49

M ax had had a long time to think about it. After he came to, face down in the parking lot with his hands cuffed behind him, he had cursed himself for his lack of attention. It was this sort of thing that got you killed... or arrested. His head throbbed from the blow that had knocked him out, but what pained him even more was that he had allowed it to happen. He had spent too long on the property and not double checked his surroundings. He had got overconfident, because up to now everything had gone his way.

He heard the crackle of a radio and a muttered conversation in Arabic. He turned his head to see two pairs of brown boots below olive green trousers. The police.

He willed himself to relax, controlling his breathing. There was no point in panicking, getting stressed. He had been caught, now he had to deal with it.

He ignored the barked questions while the cops searched him, emptying his pockets, then manhandled him roughly into the back of an SUV. In the station he remained silent while they processed him and had a medic tend to the cut on the back of his head. There was still a dull throbbing radiating from the wound to his temples, but it was nothing he hadn't dealt with before.

He used the time to think. To think about how he could turn the situation to his advantage. No-one knew who he was and as long as he remained silent, they would have difficulty in finding anything out. The arresting constable made a clumsy attempt to interrogate him, and Max ignored him, concentrating on his breathing, going within, maintaining an aura of calm. He relaxed completely, allowing his subconscious to come up with a solution. It was only when the more senior officer entered the room, the Major, when his plan solidified.

He'd had to wait, the time passing slowly, his stomach growling with hunger, before Colonel Hakim Al-Hamadi entered the room. He was tall, around six feet in height, and slim, just a slight thickening around the waist visible in his well fitting uniform. His beard was trimmed neatly, a slight peppering of grey around his temples giving him a distinguished air. However, dark smudges under his eyes and a visibly pulsing muscle in his jaw hinted at fatigue. He frowned at Max, and a flash of anger crossed his face when Max asked him to sit down.

The anger vanished, though, once Max mentioned the payments and the photographs. Instead, an expression of deep regret filled his eyes, followed by resignation, and his shoulders slumped.

"I can help you," Max repeated.

After the obvious confusion, Hakim asked, "What do you mean?"

Max leaned forward again, shielding his mouth from view, and said in a low voice. "All I want is Liam Mulroney. Let me put an end to him and your problems will go away."

Hakim blinked in confusion, his eyes roaming Max's face. "And how will you do that? You're under arrest and you are asking a policeman, a senior police officer, to do something illegal."

Max gave a wry grin. "I don't think you should lecture me on what is legal and illegal."

Hakim's eye twitched, and his frown deepened.

Max continued, "We both know Liam Mulroney is a criminal. He runs an international drug empire on your doorstep. From properties here in Dubai." Max spread his hands wide, not worrying about hiding his mouth anymore. "We're both adults. We both know a lot of..." he grinned, "alleged criminals make Dubai their home. But...." This time he leaned forward, shielding his face again, "you have been receiving a sizeable monthly payment from him for several years. For what? Sharing information? Turning a blind eye?"

Hakim didn't reply.

"So you, a man who is supposed to be upholding the law, are helping someone to break it."

Hakim looked as if he was about to say something, and Max stopped him with a raised hand. "I also know he has quite a gallery of photos of you in compromising positions, so giving you the benefit of the doubt, maybe you didn't want it to be this way." Max nodded at the three gold stars on Hakim's epaulette. "You're a senior officer. I'm sure you got there by doing a good job. I'm sure you wouldn't want any of this information to be made public. Your career would be destroyed."

Hakim stared back, not saying anything.

"And what would your wife think?" Max didn't know if Hakim was married or not, but the pain in Hakim's eyes was a dead giveaway.

"Who are you?" Hakim asked eventually.

"Just think of me as someone who can fix two of your problems at once."

"Why would you do that?"

Max sighed and looked around the room, searching for the right words. Finally, he looked back at Hakim and said, "I've also made mistakes in my life. But I want a chance to put things right. To even up the scales. 'Except for those who repent, believe and do righteous work. For them, Allah will replace their evil deeds with good. And ever is Allah forgiving and merciful.' *Sadaqallahul Azim.*"

"Ameen." Hakim dipped his head respectfully. *"Surah al-Furan."* He sighed. "A *surah* I try to live by."

"Inshallah."

"As god wills," Hakim repeated. "But it's not so easy."

Max leaned forward. "I don't judge what you've done. But I'm giving you the opportunity to make things right." It was a gamble, but Max sensed Hakim was not a bad person. He pressed on. "I'm a resourceful man. I have certain skills. I can make your problem go away. But you need to trust me."

Hakim regarded Max with suspicion. "Are you responsible for the attack on the villa? The sinking of his boat?"

Max remained silent, his face giving nothing away.

Hakim pushed his chair back. "I need to think about this."

"As you wish," Max replied. He watched Hakim stand and walk toward the door. Hakim stopped by the door and looked back at Max for a long moment. Finally, he gave a brief nod and walked out.

50

B y the time Omar knocked on the door, Hakim had been sitting in his office staring at the wall for almost an hour.

He had ignored the repeated calls from Liam on his burner phone, eventually with irritation, turning the phone off and tossing it into his desk drawer.

It had taken him a long time to decide. It was risky, but then doing nothing came with its own risks. Either way, could destroy his life and his career. But if he took the path he had decided upon, he felt like he was regaining some sort of control with a chance of getting his old life back.

When he heard the knock on the door, he took a deep breath, then swivelled in his chair to face the door.

"Come in."

Omar poked his head through the doorway. "Sir, you asked to see me?"

Hakim arranged a smile on his face and beckoned the young major in. "Yes, Omar, come in."

He gestured toward the chairs in front of his desk. "Take a seat."

Without waiting for an answer, he picked up his phone, waited a beat, then said, "Two coffees, please." He placed the phone back on the desk and watched Omar settle into his chair. The young man looked tired. He'd been working long hours ever since the attack on Liam's villa and had been on duty since the early hours of that morning.

"You were right, sir."

"About?" Hakim raised an eyebrow.

"The Range Rover. We traced the VIN. It's registered to Desert Horizon Holdings LLC, a company owned by Liam Mulroney. It's the same one that was reported stolen last week."

Hakim nodded. He was only half listening, mentally rehearsing what he would need to say as Omar continued.

"We've spoken to Liam Mulroney's staff, but all they said is he's out of the country and even they have been having trouble contacting him."

Hakim nodded, still letting Omar's words wash over him. There was another knock on the door and Omar stopped in mid-flow and looked over his shoulder as the door opened and a constable walked in with a tray containing two small ceramic coffee cups and a long spouted coffee pot.

"Thank you, Farouk. Close the door behind you, please." Hakim waited until the door had closed before picking up the *dallah*, the coffee pot, and half filling each of the small ceramic cups.

"Here. I'm sure you need this. You had an early start."

Omar smiled his thanks, picked up the cup, waited for Hakim to do the same, then took a sip.

Hakim sipped his own, his eyes on Omar, then placed his cup down on the table. He took a deep breath, then said, "Our prisoner."

"Sir?"

"There are some things going on which I can't explain, Omar."

Omar looked puzzled, and he placed his cup down. "Like what, sir? What did he say when you asked me to turn off the recording?"

Hakim nodded conspiratorially. He lowered his voice and leaned forward slightly. "Exactly Omar. That's what I'm talking about. Unfortunately, this....." He paused for effect, "goes way beyond you and me. There are some things that I'm not permitted to share with you."

Omar blinked, his eyes widening.

Hakim felt a trace of guilt, misleading the young man who had faithfully served him for years. But he had to continue.

"The work that man is doing is very important and we will have to...." He spread his hands and looked around the room as if searching in his office for the words he needed. "We will have to bend a few rules, do a few things that go against procedure. To help him and the people he represents, to get their work done."

Omar was nodding thoughtfully. "I knew there was something different about him. He had no fear and even though his Arabic is fluent, there was something about his accent."

Hakim nodded as if he agreed.

Omar leaned closer, lowering his voice, "Is he working for a foreign security service?"

Hakim shrugged while sticking out his lower lip.

"I knew it!" Omar exclaimed and slapped the table with his hand before sitting back in his chair, an excited look on his face. "It's a foreign operation against the Mulroneys. Good! It's time these foreign criminals stopped treating

Dubai as their playground. So what do you want me to do, sir?"

Hakim pursed his lips. He hadn't thought he would get this far, but now he had, he had to play it carefully.

"This conversation stays in this room, Omar. I'm trusting you and you only."

Omar beamed. "Thank you, sir. I won't let you down."

"I know you won't, Omar. That's why I chose you." Again, Hakim felt the twinge of guilt. "We need to be very careful. I don't know if the Mulroney's or their associates have eyes in here or not, but let's assume the worst. Let's keep them guessing. I'm going to arrange a transfer to Al-Wathba. I'll handle the paperwork, but I want you to personally handle the transfer."

Omar frowned. "But how will locking him in a maximum security prison help the operation?"

Hakim reached for the *dallah* and topped up Omar's cup. "That's because, Omar, he will not reach the prison."

A smile spread across Omar's face. "So you want me to divert the transport somewhere on the way?" He reached for his coffee cup and took a swig. He licked his lips and nodded. "An excellent plan, sir."

Hakim drained his cup, feeling the strong black liquid slide down his throat and sending an almost simultaneous jolt to his bloodstream. He placed the cup carefully on the desktop.

"Give me an hour to get the paperwork sorted, Omar. In the meantime, make sure our prisoner is comfortable."

Omar set his coffee cup down, pushed back his chair, and stood to attention. "Leave it to me, sir." He snapped a smart salute before spinning on his heel and walking out of the room.

Hakim exhaled loudly, releasing the tension he'd been holding without realising and allowed himself a small nod of satisfaction. That had gone much better than expected.

51

Max wiped his lips with the back of his hand and then pushed the tray away from him. There was still no sign of Hakim, but judging by the change in his treatment, things were progressing in the right direction. He'd been brought several cups of very strong coffee and then a tray laden with freshly baked bread, *hummus* and *foul medames*. It hadn't been the best he'd eaten and the Major, who had introduced himself as Omar, had apologised, explaining the police kitchen wasn't very good. Max didn't mind; he hadn't eaten since the day before, and any food in front of him was welcome—hunger being the best seasoning.

Though he was still chained to the table, the camera had remained off. He had lost track of time since his wristwatch was confiscated when he was arrested. He could have been there for minutes or hours, but the fullness of his bladder suggested it was the latter.

The waiting didn't bother Max. He'd done all he could, all he could do now was wait. And waiting was easy for him. He'd spent hours, days even, holed up in abandoned buildings in Gaza and the West Bank, with nothing to pass the time with but his thoughts. Back then, he'd daydreamed about life on the outside, when he was no longer a soldier. He'd thought about the countries he'd visit, the places he'd see, the girls he'd meet. Later, when he worked as security for the guru Atman, he'd used the guru's teachings to go within, to slow his breathing and meditate, revelling in an inner peace he had never found when he'd been a soldier.

He did the same now, closing his eyes and relaxing every part of his body, taking slow, deep breaths. After a while, he visualized a ball of light sending healing energy to the back of his head, feeling a tingling sensation as his body began to heal.

It felt like only moments had passed when he heard the door creak open and footsteps entering the room. With some effort, he brought himself back, moving his fingers and toes to regain awareness of his body before finally opening his eyes.

The young major, Omar, stood in front of him, an expression of almost reverential awe on his face.

Max raised an eyebrow.

"We're moving you."

Max nodded but remained silent as Omar stepped forward and unlocked the handcuff securing Max to the table.

Max rubbed his wrist, the skin chafed from the hand-cuffs that had been fastened tight by the overzealous constable.

"I'm sorry, you will have to wear these," Omar apologised as he held out another set of cuffs. "It's just for appearances."

Max extended his wrists.

Omar made a gesture of apology with his mouth. "Behind your back."

Max stared at him until Omar broke eye contact. Then, he pushed back his chair, stood up, and turned around, placing his hands behind his back. He didn't like the uncertainty of the situation, but it was beyond his control. Judging by the food, the coffee, and the respectful treatment he had received, something seemed to be working in his favor. He felt the cold steel of the handcuffs click shut around his wrists, followed by Omar's voice behind him.

"I've kept them as loose as I can."

"Shukraan," Max replied as he rolled his shoulders back and shook out his legs, getting the blood flowing again after sitting for so long. "What time is it?"

"Six thirty."

"Evening?"

"Yes."

Max sighed. That explained why his bladder was so full. He'd been in custody for over twelve hours.

"This way, please." Omar opened the door, and taking Max gently by the elbow, guided him out into the corridor.

"Not long now," Omar murmured and led him down the corridor.

52

H akim stepped out of the station, opened the rear doors of the van, climbed in, and immediately closed the doors behind him.

Seated inside on the steel bench seat that ran the length of the van was a single man, his left hand secured by a handcuff attached to the steel bar that ran above the seat.

Hakim moved further inside and sat on the opposite bench seat. He studied the prisoner, who looked remarkably unfazed by his lengthy detention.

"How do I know I can trust you?"

"You don't," came the reply.

Hakim chewed his lip.

"But you have to choose one of us. It's me or Liam Mulroney. I'm not the one blackmailing you. I'm offering to help you."

Hakim stared back at him. The man seemed relaxed, confident, not the usual demeanour of a prisoner handcuffed to a police van.

"You've seen what I can do," the man continued.

"That's what worries me. I don't want more shootouts,

more dead bodies. I don't want properties being destroyed. Dubai has a reputation for law and order. Millions of tourists come here every year knowing they can have a safe holiday."

"And billions of dollars of ill-gotten gains are laundered through the economy too every year. By many of your residents."

Hakim grimaced. The man had a point. He looked around the van, the sterile interior, the glaring white overhead light reflecting off the stainless steel fittings. "Can you promise me there will be no more dead bodies?"

"No," the man replied immediately. "But I can assure you that no innocent lives will be lost. As you have seen so far. I'm sure you've looked into the background of the men who were killed. None of them were saints."

"No," Hakim agreed, glancing down at the manila envelope in his right hand. He took a deep breath, realizing it was time to take a stand. He tossed the envelope onto the seat across from him. "Your wristwatch and the other items you had are all in there. Unfortunately, we'll need to keep the Range Rover."

He stood, removed a set of keys from his pocket and unlocked the handcuffs. Sitting back down, he said, "I'm going to trust you. I want Liam Mulroney removed from my life. I truly hope you're the man to do it."

The man nodded. "I am."

"Hmmm." Hakim hoped he had made the right choice. He wasn't one to gamble, but desperation had pushed him. "Liam Mulroney is demanding I hand you over. I'm not inclined to do so, which means he can't know I've let you go." He gestured toward the van's interior. "This van is officially transporting you to Al-Wathba, a high-security prison in Abu Dhabi. Unofficially, you won't make it there. My man will drop you in a remote location, out of sight. From there, it's up to you to find your way. I'm sure you'll manage."

The man gave a nod and then asked, "And who does your man, the young major, think I am?"

Hakim allowed himself a smile for the first time. "He thinks you are an agent for a foreign security service tasked with bringing down the Mulroney empire. I've no idea what gave him that idea."

The man opposite him smiled. "The result will be the same."

"Good." Hakim nodded at the manila envelope still lying untouched on the bench seat. "There's a burner phone in there. My number is on it. There's a limit to what I can do for you, but I'll try. All I ask is that you'll be discrete and to keep me informed."

"I can do that."

Hakim nodded, his gaze dropping to the floor. He had crossed a line from which there was no turning back. "He's in Oman," he said, looking up with resolve. "Muscat. I traced his phone. The location is in the envelope." He leaned forward slightly. "Whatever you need to do, do it there. There's been more than enough chaos here in the last week for me to handle."

"Okay."

Hakim sighed. "I'm not a bad man. I do my job to the best of my ability." He looked at the man, hoping for some sympathy. It wasn't clear in his expression, but he pressed on, "I made a mistake—taking his money was a moment of weakness, one I've regretted ever since." He shook his head, his gaze dropping to the floor once more. "As for the photos... another weakness, another regret."

Raising his eyes, he locked onto the man's gaze with intensity. "I love my wife. I love my daughters. They mean the world to me. If you can do what you say you can do, I promise I will never stray again."

The man stared back at him, the intensity of his gaze unnerving, and Hakim had to look away, finding the floor with his eyes, as a profound sense of regret washed over him.

He felt a hand on his arm and flinched. The man had moved closer and was looking at him earnestly.

"Every saint has a past, and every sinner has a future. We all make mistakes. Mine are worse than yours, but someone told me once, someone I respect, that it's never too late to make a change. The important thing is to make that change. That's up to you, Hakim."

Hakim swallowed and nodded. *"Inshallah,"* he muttered.

"Yes, *inshallah*, Hakim, but you have to do something about it too." The man gripped his arm and grinned. "Even Allah needs something to work with."

Hakim looked into the man's eyes and felt hope.

"Thank you. *Allah yuwafiq*, may God grant you success."

The man nodded, releasing his grip on Hakim's arm, and leaned back against the side wall of the van. Hakim took a step toward the rear door, pausing with one hand resting on the handle. He turned his head slightly, glancing back. "What do I call you?" he asked.

The man smiled. "You can call me, Max."

"Max," Hakim frowned. "Max," he repeated. "That's not an Arab name."

Max winked, but said nothing.

Hakim stared at him for a moment longer, then climbed out of the van. He closed the doors behind him, then banged twice on the side of the van with the flat of his hand. The van's engine rumbled into life and pulled away from the station.

Hakim stood with his hands on his hips, watching the van pull out onto the road and merge with the passing traffic. "Max," he said again, then turned and entered the station.

He failed to notice the white Nissan Patrol pulling away from the curb.

53

Barry spat a mouthful of tepid coffee out the window. "Motherfucker!" he cursed, crunching the disposable coffee cup in his fist. He tossed it into the passenger footwell and reached for the binoculars lying on the seat beside him. Adjusting the focus, he zeroed in on the man being escorted into the back of the police van.

It was definitely him.

What the hell was going on? Barry clenched his teeth and tightened his grip on the binoculars. What was that cop up to? That lying bastard. Liam had promised that Hakim would release the prisoner to them, and Barry had been waiting outside the station for the call. But the call never came, and the longer he waited, the more suspicious he grew. He already distrusted cops, especially the corrupt ones who took his money. To Barry, anyone who didn't stick to their principles was untrustworthy. You became a cop to uphold the law—if you compromised that, you were worthless.

By mid afternoon, hot sticky and increasingly irritated, he had placed another call to Liam for an update, but Liam, sounding irritated himself, had said he had nothing to report and, in fact, Hakim wasn't taking his calls.

Barry had a bad feeling, and when he saw the prisoner being moved into a transport van, his suspicions deepened. The cop got into the front of the van, but it didn't move. As time dragged on, Barry grew more and more frustrated. Everything was getting on his nerves—the heat, the lack of action, the noise of traffic passing by. He started his car, rolled up the windows, and cranked up the air conditioning, finally feeling some relief as the cool air chilled his sweat-soaked shirt and muffled the outside noise. He knew he needed to calm down—nothing good ever came from acting out of anger. Forcing himself to relax, he rested the binoculars on his lap, keeping his eyes fixed on the van.

Around ten minutes after the prisoner emerged, he spied the familiar tall slim figure of Colonel Hakim walking out of the station. He raised the binoculars and watched as Hakim climbed into the back of the van. "What the fuck are you doing, Hakim?" Barry muttered. Why would a senior police officer be climbing into the back of a van transporting a prisoner? Something definitely wasn't right.

The van still didn't move. Barry shook his head. The cops were up to something. He tapped his fingers impatiently on the steering wheel, thinking through his options. He didn't want to go to the station himself. He was pretty sure they had nothing on him, but he didn't trust the cops to leave him alone. Besides, the longer they didn't know he was in Dubai, the better. He could call Liam and fill him in, but if Hakim wasn't answering Liam's calls, what was the point? Barry preferred to handle problems before Liam even knew they existed, and he wasn't about to stop now.

He stopped tapping the steering wheel and narrowed his eyes as the rear door of the van opened. Quickly reaching for the binoculars, he raised them to his eyes and watched Hakim climb out and close the door behind him. The cop banged the side of the van twice and Barry saw the lights come on and the van move through the parking lot toward the road. Barry dropped the binoculars onto the seat beside him and fastened his seatbelt. He waited for the van to pull out into the traffic before selecting drive and following after it.

54

M ax stretched his legs out and thought over the conversation he'd had before the van got moving. Hakim seemed like a good man, albeit hampered by poor decisions in the past. That's okay. Max had been the same. What was important was that he was being released, but even more important was that he now knew where Liam Mulroney was.

He ripped the top off the manila envelope and emptied the contents onto the seat beside him. He picked up his G-shock, fastened it around his wrist and checked the time. Almost seven pm. It had been a long day.

There was a cheap mobile phone, as Hakim promised, and he tapped on the screen. The contact list contained a single number with the letter H beside it. Max slipped the phone into his pocket, then picked up the folded slip of paper.

There was a single typed line—a set of co-ordinates. Max nodded. Hakim had delivered. He refolded the paper and slipped it into his pocket. Closing his eyes, he settled back against the wall of the van. There was nothing he could do now but wait for the journey to end.

It was around thirty minutes later when he felt the van slow. Max guessed by the speed and the sound of other vehicles that they had been on a motorway for some time, but it was only a guess. There were no windows in the van and he was purely going by the sound and vibrations felt through the side of the van.

The van slowed significantly, took a turn, then proceeded slowly for another minute or so before coming to a complete stop. He then heard a beeping sound as the van reversed and then stopped again. The engine was turned off, and he heard a door open and close up front. He sat up and turned to face the door.

The door opened, revealing the smiling face of the Major. "You can get out here," he said.

Max slid along the bench seat, then stood and dropped out of the rear of the van onto the tarmac. It was dark, but beyond the van he could see a floodlit service station and beyond that the lights and roar of traffic on the motorway. The van was parked in a corner, far from the lights behind a row of parked semi-trailers.

"We are at the Al-Samhah service station about halfway between Dubai and Abu Dhabi."

Max nodded as he looked around.

"Do you have someone who can pick you up?" the Major asked, then apologised. "Sorry, of course you will. You'll have a team here." He grinned. "I'm honoured to have been a part of your mission. I'll be watching the news headlines for when your mission is a success." He finished with a wink.

Max nodded conspiratorially. "Thank you for your

help." He reached out and shook the young man's hand. "It won't go unnoticed."

The Major beamed. "*Bil tawfiq.* Good luck."

Max nodded his thanks and remained where he was as Omar climbed back into the front of the van. He waited until the van had pulled away before making his way across the parking lot toward the service station. The first order of business was to empty his bladder, then he'd call Azar to pick him up.

55

The toilet was like motorway toilets all over the world. Grimy, cracked tiles, and an overwhelming smell of disinfectant and urine.

Max ignored it all, feeling great relief as he emptied his bladder into the urinal. He had just finished and was zipping himself up when he heard the creak of the door as someone walked in. He turned to move toward the washbasin and saw a large man in the doorway, a Glock held in a two handed grip pointed at his head.

Max recognised him. He'd seen him before. At Liam Mulroney's villa. His right-hand man. The Glock had a suppressor on the barrel, the man's finger on the trigger. He looked tired and unwashed, several days' stubble on his jaw, his hair greasy, and his clothes creased. All this Max registered in a second, even before the man spoke.

"Who the fuck are you?" the man growled in a thick Irish accent.

Max didn't answer, his brain making calculations. There were four empty toilet cubicles to his left, four urinals to his right. Three washbasins closer to the door. The door was closed, and the man was about three metres from him.

"Are ya deaf?" he growled again. "Do you speak fuckin' English?"

Max said nothing. Adrenaline coursing through his system, he slowly moved his weight to the balls of his feet, ready to spring into action. He ignored the Glock, instead fixing his gaze on the man's eyes.

There was a shift in the man's gaze, the Glock moved slightly and his finger squeezed the trigger. Max flinched involuntarily as the Glock coughed. He felt the parting of air as a round passed the side of his head and shattered a tile in the wall behind him.

"The next one will be in your knee. Fucking answer me."

Max thought fast. He needed to say something, do something. He held up his hands, arranging his face in what he hoped was a panicked expression. "Please, please, don't shoot. I'm only an employee," he said. "You don't want me. You want my boss."

The man nodded, his glare changing to a satisfied smirk. "And who is your boss?"

Max stuttered, "I... I.... I'll tell you. But please don't shoot me. I'm not paid enough to get shot."

"You fuckers are all the same," the man scoffed. "No balls and no fucking loyalty. But it suits me."

Max nodded eagerly.

"So tell me."

Max shook his head. "No, no, not here. What if someone comes in? I don't want to go to prison again."

The man frowned with suspicion. "Okay," he nodded slowly. "But that's something else you need to explain. How those bastards let you go!"

Again Max nodded eagerly. "Even I don't understand, but I'm not going to argue with them."

The man scowled, then stepped to one side and, with a jerk of the Glock, indicated to Max that he should move toward the door.

Max lowered his hands slightly and took a step forward. There was a creak, and the door swung open, revealing a middle-aged truck driver who in mid stride noticed Max standing with his hands in the air. At the same time, Max ducked down and lunged forward.

Liam's man, momentarily distracted, was a split second late in reacting, causing the round he fired to pass harmlessly over Max's head. Seizing the opportunity, Max grasped the wrist holding the Glock with his left hand and twisted it sharply upwards. Another shot rang out, tearing into the ceiling and sending a shower of plaster raining down. The big man, exhibiting impressive strength, slammed his free hand into Max's shoulder, forcing him back and down.

Max couldn't relinquish his grip on the Glock. Using his bodyweight, he yanked the gun arm down and to the side, throwing the man off balance. In the same fluid motion, he twisted and delivered an elbow strike aimed at the man's face, targeting his nose. There was the crunch of cartilage and an anguished gasp as blood sprayed from his shattered nose. He staggered back a step, rage filling his eyes.

Before Max could press his advantage, the man barrelled into him, using his full weight to force Max back against the washbasins. The edge of the basin caught Max in the spine, and pain surged through his body like an electric shock. The Glock fell from both their hands and clattered across the floor tiles. The man swung a meaty fist at

Max's head, but he deflected it with his forearm, the impact rattling his body.

Max countered, grabbing the man's head with both his hands and forcing a knee into his gut. He grunted but didn't fall. His hands grasped Max's arm, and he twisted, using his bodyweight to hurl Max against the stalls. The air left Max's body, and he froze momentarily as the big man rushed him, ducking at the last minute and the man crashed his fist against the metal frame of the stall. He howled in pain as the bones in his fist cracked, and Max punched him hard in the solar plexus with his right, then aimed another blow at the man's throat.

He missed the throat, but the blow to the solar plexus stunned the man, leaving him gasping and slow in his movements. The man retaliated with a wild punch, but Max easily evaded it, countering with a right cross to the man's jaw. The impact whipped the man's head to the side, and Max stepped forward, slamming the side of his foot into the man's knee. A sickening pop echoed as the man howled, dropping to one knee.

Desperately, the man grasped for Max's leg, pulling him down as they both crashed to the floor. Max struck again with the point of his elbow before twisting free and rolling on top of him. With one hand, he gripped the man's hair, yanking his head back, while his other arm wrapped around the man's neck, locking his forearm in place and squeezing tightly.

The man flung his head back, trying to strike Max with the back of his skull, but Max, anticipating the move, shifted his face aside and tightened his grip around the man's neck. The man's breath faltered as he struggled, trying to pry Max's arm loose with his free hand. Max held firm, squeezing with all his strength. The man's struggles gradually weakened, and after what felt like an eternity, he finally went limp.

Max held on a moment longer to be certain, then released him, pushing himself to his feet. He stood bent double, gasping for breath as adrenaline surged through him, his hands trembling. Blood dripped from somewhere on his face, and as the adrenaline began to fade, pain radiated through his body, particularly from his ribs and head. Bending down, he retrieved the Glock from the floor, then checked the man's pulse—it was faint, but still there.

Max took a breath. He couldn't leave him alive. He went through the man's wallet, removing a wallet, a set of car keys, and a phone, then straightened up, raised the Glock and fired a round into the back of the man's head. Turning away, he glimpsed himself in the mirror. His lower lip was split, blood trickling down his chin. He was bleeding from his left nostril and his right eye was swelling. But he was alive.

He took one last look at the body on the floor, a pool of thick crimson blood spreading out from the head, then carefully opened the toilet door.

There was no sign of the truck driver.

56

Outside, Max scanned the parking lot, Glock in hand, but there was no one in sight. Liam's guy must have come alone, and word of the fight had clearly spread—not a single customer in sight. Slipping the Glock into his waistband, he pressed the button on the key fob, hearing a beep and seeing the lights flash on a white Nissan Patrol. He hurried over, jumped in, started the engine, and sped out of the service station onto the highway. Once he was in the flow of traffic, he pulled out the burner phone Hakim had given him and dialed his number.

"Your call has come sooner than I hoped." Hakim didn't sound happy. "Why....?"

"There's a dead body you need to clean up," Max interrupted. "In the service station bathroom. As soon as your guy left, I was jumped by Liam's man. Big guy. Irish. One sec." Max wedged the phone between his ear and his shoulder, wincing as the movement reminded him of his injuries. He opened the wallet. "It says here Bairrfhionn Aodhán Fitzpatrick."

Max heard a muttered curse then, "I know him. He's Liam's second in command."

"Yeah, well, he's not anymore. You'll need to get the place cleaned up. There was a witness too."

Max heard another curse.

Max tossed the wallet onto the seat beside him and glanced up into the mirror, catching sight of his battered face. "It was self-defence, Hakim. He came after me."

He heard Hakim grunt.

"How did he know where I was, Hakim? Can you trust your man? What's his name? Omar?"

"With my life!" Hakim shot back, indignation clear in his voice.

Max frowned. "Okay," he said, pausing to think. There was either a leak in Hakim's station, or he had been followed from there. Either way, it didn't change the situation. "Well, it doesn't matter now." He saw a sign for the next exit and changed lanes. "I'll give you the benefit of the doubt, Hakim. Don't disappoint me."

There was a lengthy silence, then Hakim replied, "You have my word."

Max took a deep breath, again wincing as pain laced through his ribs. He glanced in the mirror as he slowed for the exit. The swelling in his right eye was getting more pronounced, the discolouration around the socket visible even in the dark. "I need to patch myself up. I'll speak soon." He ended the call without waiting for an answer, then took the exit off the motorway and headed back to Dubai.

57

Hakim closed his eyes and pinched the bridge of his nose. A dull ache throbbed in his temples, and there was an uneasy feeling in his upper chest. He took a deep breath, then opened his eyes and stared at the wrecked service station bathroom. The door of one stall hung lopsidedly on its hinge. Two mirrors were cracked and there were shattered wall tiles and a hole in the false ceiling. But worse than that was the body of a large western male lying at his feet, a pool of congealed blood surrounding his head like a crimson halo.

Hakim's nose twitched at the smell, a unique combination of blood, stale urine, disinfectant, and propellant.

He counted three spent shell casings amongst the debris of broken tiles, and ceiling plaster, but there was no sign of the weapon.

Sighing loudly, he turned and shot a heavy look at Omar, who hovered uncomfortably in the doorway, then pushed past him and stood outside. He wished he could rewind to a week ago, when his life had seemed so much more peaceful, less complicated. In fact, he wished he could rewind even further, to his life before Liam Mulroney.

"I'm sorry, sir, I don't know how he knew."

Hakim shook his head. "It doesn't matter now." He nodded at the waiting paramedics and then, with a jerk of his head, indicated to Omar that he should move aside. The flashing lights of the emergency vehicles filled the sky, and several of his men busied themselves taking witness statements from the truck drivers and service station staff.

He beckoned Omar closer and lowered his voice, "Make sure you get all the security camera footage. There can be no record of this. Otherwise, the entire operation will be compromised."

Omar nodded and gulped.

"And bring me the witness statements when they're done."

Again, Omar nodded unhappily.

Hakim glanced at his watch. He had promised Latifah he'd be home an hour ago to put the girls to bed. *"Ibn al kalb!* Son of a dog!" he cursed aloud.

Omar flinched at the uncharacteristic outburst. "I'm sorry, sir. I didn't tell anyone."

"I know Omar, I know." He turned to face him. "Let's hope, for both our sakes, that this man is successful in his mission. Otherwise..." he trailed off, the meaning in his words clear to Omar, who grimaced and looked down at the ground. Hakim meant it. The sooner Liam Mulroney and his organisation was wiped from the earth, the better.

He felt his phone buzz in his pocket. He pulled it out and looked at the name on the screen. Speak of the devil. He groaned inwardly.

"See to the camera footage. I need to take this."

Omar nodded and walked away as Hakim held the phone to his ear.

"Alo."

58

L iam hung up, a growing sense of unease taking over.

He was certain Hakim was hiding something. He'd told him that his hands were tied, that his superiors were now involved, and that there was little he could do. Frustrated, Liam had lost his temper, screaming down the phone at Hakim. He'd even threatened to leak the photographs, even though he was still reluctant to do so right now. Once the photos were leaked, any leverage he had over the Colonel was gone. Hakim had promised to keep trying, to find a way, but Liam's gut told him something was off.

He stared at the phone in his hand while he thought about what to do next. Adding to his unease was the fact that he hadn't heard from Barry for the best part of the day. That was highly unusual. He dialled his number again, put the phone on speaker and walked over to the window of his study and stared out across the floodlit lawn as the phone rang out.

The Saudis had arrived earlier in the day, their dusty white Land Cruiser now parked facing the gate, ready for a quick evacuation if necessary.

So far they had impressed Liam, quickly taking control of the security, organising shifts and assessing the weak points of the compound. They had brought weapons too and one man was now pacing up and down by the gate, an M4 assault rifle cradled in his arms. With the Saudis, he now had five men watching the house. Five well trained and heavily armed men. No-one would get through them.

He turned his attention back to the phone as it rang out unanswered and Liam's frown deepened. It was the third time he'd called and again, there had been no response from Barry. He typed a brief message: *Call me when you're free*, then slipped the phone back into his pocket.

He walked over to the bar and poured himself three fingers of whiskey from the crystal decanter. Taking a large gulp, he swallowed it quickly, then stared blankly at the glass in his hand. He'd been drinking more than usual, and ever since fleeing the house in Dubai, he hadn't worked out. But he kept telling himself that once this was over, everything would change. He'd get back to his routine, rebuild his life and business. Maybe he'd take more time off, enjoy the fruits of his labor. Take the boat out more often. The thought of his beloved boat stirred the anger he was trying to hold back. "Bastard," he muttered, then downed another swig of whiskey.

The buzz of an incoming message on his phone interrupted his thoughts, and he set the glass down and retrieved his phone.

A message from Barry. *Can't talk now. Working on something. Will report soon.*

Liam felt an immediate sense of relief. Good old Barry. He could always depend on the man. Feeling a little better, Liam reached for the decanter and topped up his glass.

Hopefully, if all went well, his life could soon return to normal.

59

M ax stared at the phone screen as he sat in the parking garage of the Royal Central Hotel. He hoped the message would buy him some time. He'd ignored the first few calls to the phone he'd taken from Barry's body, hoping by doing so that Liam Mulroney would assume his man was busy. But when the third call had come in, just as he was parking the stolen Nissan Patrol, he knew he had to do something. He needed Liam to think everything was normal for as long as possible.

The phone buzzed in his hand.

Keep me posted.

Good. He nodded with satisfaction. It had worked. For now.

He climbed out of the Nissan and made his way over to the elevator. When it arrived, he walked in, grimacing at the sight of his battered face in the mirror. His shirt was also ripped, but fortunately the blood was not showing on his black shirt. Now Max was back in the relative safety of his hotel, his body began to break down, exhaustion combined with pain filling his body. He hadn't slept for almost twenty-four hours, and his body had taken a beating. He needed protein, pain killers and sleep, preferably in that order.

He pressed the button for his floor and prayed no-one would get in on the way. He looked like he'd gone three rounds with Conor McGregor and lost.

Fortunately, the elevator only stopped once it reached his floor, and once in his room, he stripped off and stood for a long time under a hot shower, the stream of hot water going some way to easing the aches and pains in his body.

Afterwards, standing naked in front of the mirror, he took stock of the damage. His right eye had swelled considerably, almost closing the eye, the bruising giving him the appearance of a panda. His lip was split and one side of his body was discoloured, the purple and blue of the bruising highlighting the white scars of his old bullet wounds. He probed his ribcage with his fingertips, but apart from tenderness, nothing appeared to be broken. He'd been lucky.

He wrapped himself in a bathrobe, then sat cross-legged on the bed, closing his eyes and sending healing energy to his body as he waited for his food to arrive.

When the doorbell rang, he called out for them to leave it outside and then waited before opening the door. The fewer people who saw him in this state, the better.

After a large steak and a handful of painkillers, he laid himself down on the bed, closed his eyes, and was fast asleep within minutes.

60

"Are you sure you're okay?" Ramesh asked, a look of concern on his face.

"I'm fine," Max flashed him a smile, although even the act of smiling was painful. He lowered himself into the chair beside Ramesh, trying not to wince, and prove his words wrong. The swelling in his eye had subsided, he was now able to open it, but the bruising remained. He removed the baseball cap he had pulled low over his head and tossed it onto the bench top and grinned. "You should see the other guy."

"Really?" Ramesh sounded doubtful.

"Yeah, he's dead."

"Oh."

Max scanned the monitors in front of Ramesh as the young Indian hacker sat in a stunned silence.

He could see the Nissan Patrol on the security camera feed where he had backed it into the loading bay. Several stock market indices scrolled continuously on another monitor, but the one directly in front of Ramesh was the most interesting. It was the satellite view of a large residen-

tial compound standing lush green in an urban area of
sandy browns and greys. In the midst of the green was a
large white villa beside a rectangular swimming pool, and a
smaller white building to one side beside the compound
wall.

"Is that....?"

"His house in Oman. I matched it against the coordinates you gave me as well as cross checked it with the list of
properties owned by Liam Mulroney. It's definitely his."

"Can you zoom in closer?"

Ramesh tapped a command on his keyboard, and the
image enlarged to fill the whole screen.

Max rolled the chair closer and studied the image. The
compound was not quite a perfect square, with just the rear
boundary slightly longer than the others. Although on a
corner plot, there was only a single point of entry.

"It's just over half an acre. He bought the land about six
years ago and built the villa. I've even got the plans,"
Ramesh added eagerly.

Max grunted an acknowledgement as he studied the
villa with narrowed eyes. The problem was the one point of
access. The main gate was bound to be guarded, which
meant the only option was coming in over the walls.

"Show me the street view."

Ramesh leaned forward, entered a command, and the
picture on the monitor changed.

Max frowned. The wall looked to be around eight feet in
height and topped with broken glass.

"Here, use this." Ramesh slid the mouse over, and Max
began changing the view, moving along the street. The gate
was steel and the same height as the walls, with a door inset
for pedestrian access. Above the gate, on each side, sat a
security camera. Max moved along the boundary to the

corner and then down the next street, before examining the neighbouring properties, trying to find a weak point. After a couple of minutes, he sat back in his chair and exhaled loudly.

"Well?" Ramesh asked.

Max stuck out his lip and shook his head. "I can't immediately see a way in. "

Ramesh nodded, scratched his head, and turned to face the monitor. "So what do we do?"

Max noted Ramesh's use of 'we' and it almost made him smile. Almost. He had located the man, but still needed to get to him. There were so many unknowns. Did he have security guards? If so, how many and what was their shift pattern? Were they armed? Were the neighbouring properties occupied? Unfortunately, the answers would not be found by looking at a computer screen.

"Zoom out on the overhead view," he instructed, and then leaned forward to study the image. After a moment, he sat back, even more frustrated. There was no cover in the street and if he sat there in a vehicle observing the property, he would stick out like a sore thumb.

"I need a drone," he said after a moment's deliberation.

"I can arrange that." Ramesh nodded eagerly.

"And I need to go to Muscat."

61

"Y̲ou'll need a four-wheel drive."

"I've got one."

"I won't ask from where," Hakim muttered.

"I wouldn't tell you."

"No." Max heard Hakim sigh. "It will take you around six hours, give or take. Best you do it at night."

Max nodded. He had planned on doing that, anyway. "Any patrols?"

"There are, but....." Max heard Hakim hesitate, and he frowned.

"I'll call in a favour. I have a friend in the border patrol. We were in the academy together. Tell me when you're going and I'll ask him to look the other way."

"He can't get me through the normal border crossing?"

"No. Too difficult. There are four thousand crossings a day. There are eyes everywhere. Cameras monitoring everything. It's better you cross through the mountains at night."

"And you can trust him?"

"I think so."

"You think so?"

Hakim sighed down the phone. "He owes me one. He should pull through."

Max made a face. He didn't like relying on others. He thought for a moment, his eyes on Ramesh, who was pretending he wasn't listening.

"Offer him something in return." Max snapped his fingers to get Ramesh's attention. "Tell him you've got a lead on a major drug trafficker. Then when this is done, you share some of the glory in bringing down Liam Mulroney and his empire."

Max waited for a reply and then Hakim said, "That will work."

"Good. Tell him I'm going tonight."

"Tonight?"

"Yes. Don't let me down, Hakim."

"I'll do my part. The rest...."

Max could almost hear Hakim shrug.

"That's all I can ask for, Hakim." Max was about to end the call when he thought he'd try his luck once more. "Actually, there's one more thing."

"I'm not sure I want to know."

"I need some weapons."

62

M ax pulled to a stop and turned the engine off. He climbed out of the Nissan Patrol and stood on the hard packed surface of the desert track. Ahead of him, he could see the lights of Route 15 and the distant hum of traffic. A line of light on the horizon signalled the arrival of a new day. He stretched his arms over his head, wincing as his body reminded him of the fight, shook out his legs and then walked around to the front of the vehicle and leaned against the hood. The air was cool and apart from the distant hum from the motorway, and the ticking of the cooling engine, it was silent. Above him, still visible in the faint light of dawn, was a glorious display of the heavens, billions of stars twinkling above him. He gazed for a moment, reveling in the universe's beauty, and took a deep breath of fresh desert air.

The crossing had gone without a hitch, Max easily finding the start of the track that led through the Hajar mountains and across the border into Oman. Hakim's coordinates had been accurate to the metre. Hakim's former classmate had obviously done his part, too. Apart from a fox he had surprised in a *wadi*, he'd not seen a single living being, no sign of the border patrols that apparently policed the area.

Max loved the desert. He'd spent a lot of time in the Negev when he'd been a soldier and grown to love the vast expanse. The harsh, unforgiving environment had a beauty all of its own, one you had to experience to understand. The vastness, the silence, the absence of humans, brought an inner peace unobtainable in other more populated environments.

As he stood gazing out over the *wadis* and foothills, he felt more relaxed than he had in weeks. Despite the daunting and dangerous task ahead, a calmness enveloped him, making him feel at one with his surroundings. He closed his eyes, taking several slow, deep breaths, allowing a sense of contentment to fill his being. If everything worked out, perhaps he could take some time away from civilization —spend a few days alone in the desert, camping among the ever-changing dunes.

He imagined exploring the twelve thousand square kilometers of the Wahiba Sands in Oman, basking in solitude, apart from the Bedouin, resting and recharging. He didn't need to return to Dubai; he had no ties, no responsibilities. He was free. A smile crept across his face as he opened his eyes. But first, he reminded himself, there was a man to kill.

63

L iam sipped on his coffee as he stared out over the swimming pool. It was getting a little too warm to be outside and if it wasn't for the shade of the olive tree, he would have already retreated indoors.

Joy moved around him, clearing the breakfast dishes, but he barely noticed. He still hadn't heard from Barry, and his concern was growing. It wasn't like his second-in-command to go silent for this long. Other than the message last night, there had been nothing. He'd expected at least a text by this morning, but so far, there was no update.

Setting his coffee mug on the table, he picked up his phone and checked for a message again—nothing. His thumb hovered over the screen before tapping redial. He put the call on speaker and listened as it rang. After a minute, it stopped. Liam shook his head. Something was wrong. He could feel it. He scrolled through his contacts and dialed Hakim. Again, the phone rang and rang, but after a minute, it cut off. He frowned and hit redial, only to get the same result. "Fucking useless..." he muttered, catching himself when he noticed Joy nearby. He bit back the rest, set the phone down, and forced himself to relax.

"Will there be anything else, sir?" Joy asked.

Liam arranged his face in a smile, took a deep breath, and turned to face her. "Just some more coffee please, Joy."

She bobbed her head and gave him a nervous smile.

Noticing her discomfort, Liam attempted to put her at ease. "The breakfast was delicious, thank you."

Her expression relaxed, and she smiled wider. "Thank you, sir. What would you like for lunch?"

Liam had no appetite, and if he was honest, had tasted nothing he'd eaten at breakfast, despite what he had told Joy. "I'll leave it up to you, Joy. I'm sure it will be delicious."

His words had the desired effect and a much happier Joy nodded, then hurried away back to the house.

Liam's smile vanished, and he clenched his teeth. Something was definitely wrong. No matter how he tried to stay positive, that neither Barry nor Hakim were answering his calls was a bad sign. His fingers curled into a fist, and he slammed it against the armrest of his chair. "Fuck, fuck, fuck," he muttered under his breath. The worst part was the uncertainty. If he knew what was happening, he could act— make decisions to regain control. But here he was, sitting by the pool, waiting for a phone call. There had to be something he could do.

He became aware of a buzzing sound and absentmindedly waved his hand near his ear. The buzzing grew louder. He waved his hand again and shook his head. "Bloody insects," he muttered. But as the sound grew louder, he realised it must be something else. Pushing his chair back, he stood up and looked around for the source of the noise. Was Abdullah trimming the grass? He turned to look at the lawn, but Abdullah was nowhere to be seen. It was then he noticed the guard beside the gate looking up at the sky, shielding his eyes with his hand.

Liam, too, looked up, trying to see what the guard was looking at. At first he didn't see it, but then there was a movement like a slow-moving bird.

"What the fuck?!"

64

"Are you getting this?"

"Crystal clear," came the voice in Max's ear.

Max sat in the rear of the Nissan Patrol, the tailgate open and the drone controller in his lap.

Ramesh had done well. The drone he'd supplied was a DJI Mavic 3 with a range of up to fifteen kilometres and a flight time of almost forty minutes. It was easy to fly. The built in stabilisation and automatic gimbal adjustments meant it only required minor corrections to keep it on course, allowing Max to concentrate on the images he could see on the screen. Ramesh was also watching via a private Facebook Live link he had set up, and was recording the footage in case Max needed to review it later.

Max crosschecked with the map on the screen of his phone and then directed the drone in a banking right turn as the road curved toward the villa. It came into view on the screen, a large compound surrounded by a white wall, the lush green of the gardens standing out in stark contrast to the less irrigated properties of the neighbours. With another adjustment, Max slowed the forward momentum of the drone as it crossed the walls and then put it into a hover above Liam Mulroney's villa. Just as in the satellite images from Google Earth, there was a sprawling single storey flat roofed villa gleaming stark white on the screen. Beside it was the turquoise blue of the swimming pool and over near the boundary wall another white two-storey building housing the staff quarters.

Max reduced the height of the drone's hover and leaned forward to peer at the screen. Liam's G-Wagen was parked to the side of the villa and there was another white Toyota Land Cruiser parked in the centre of the driveway facing the gate. A man sat by the swimming pool, and Max lowered the drone a little more so he could get a better view. The man pushed back his chair and stood up and appeared to be looking around. Ramesh had told him the drone was quieter than most, but it obviously wasn't quiet enough because the man looked up into the sky and Max recognised him instantly. Liam Mulroney.

Liam Mulroney stood looking up at the drone and, for Max, it was almost as if he was looking directly at him.

"He's seen it," Ramesh's voice once again appeared in Max's ear.

"Yeah." Max sighed. "That didn't take long." Max wasn't concerned about being found. He had launched the drone from two kilometres away, but had hoped the drone wouldn't be spotted so soon.

"Raise it up."

"There's no point now," Max muttered, as he watched Liam walk away from the swimming pool and toward the front gate. There was another man by the gate and as he stepped away, walking closer to Liam, Max spotted the assault rifle cradled in his arms.

"He's armed," Ramesh gasped excitedly.

"Yup," Max muttered, and lowered the height of the drone again.

"What are you doing?"

"Getting a closer look."

Liam was now gesticulating in the air, arguing with the armed guard. Max could see the weapon now. It looked like an M4 Carbine.

Another man appeared from the staff quarters. He, too, was armed, and he looked up at the drone before sprinting across to join the two men in the driveway. Max moved the drone in a slow circle, the men turning to watch it, then the newcomer raised his weapon and aimed it at the drone.

"Look out," Ramesh shouted, but Max was already moving the drone, increasing the height rapidly. There was a flash from the muzzle of the weapon, another M4, and Max moved the drone sideways. He didn't think the guards would have any hope of hitting the drone without a shotgun, but for the sake of safety he increased the height again, at the same time watching the first guard put his hand on the shooter's arm and stop him from shooting.

They appeared to be arguing.

Max grinned.

65

T he two men were arguing in Arabic, and Liam couldn't follow what they were saying. He didn't care though, his attention firmly on the drone that hovered high above them, barely visible now against the glare of the sky.

His ears were still ringing from the gunshot fired near his head. He hoped the neighbors hadn't noticed, but his worry about the police was overshadowed by a bigger question—who the hell was flying that drone? How had they found him? What did they want? The anger he'd been holding back since he arrived finally erupted into a full-blown rage. "Who the fuck are you?" he yelled at the sky, raising his hand to give the drone the middle finger. "Fuck you, fuck you, fuck you!"

The drone didn't move, and he realised the men had stopped arguing. He turned and grabbed the assault rifle from the nearest man, Hassan, and attempted to wrestle it from his hands. Hassan didn't let go, anxiously glancing at Khalid for support. Khalid stepped closer and placed a hand on Liam's arm. He locked eyes with Liam and said, "Sir, no. Let it go."

Reluctantly, Liam let go, still seething with anger, and stared back up at the drone as Khalid continued. "It will be very difficult to shoot it down and if we do, the gunshots will attract too much attention. I'm sure you don't want the police around."

Khalid was right, but that didn't help Liam's anger. He needed to take action. He wished Barry were here—Barry always knew what to do in moments like this. Liam pulled his phone from his pocket and dialed Barry's number. Holding the phone to his ear, he glared at the drone, tuning out the hushed conversation between his guards. The gunshot had already drawn the other men, all armed and ready. As the phone rang unanswered, Liam glanced back at the house. Joy and Grace stood at the window, watching, while Abdullah lingered by the garage. As much as Liam hated to admit it, if one gunshot drew this much attention, he dreaded the fallout if they fired again. The phone rang out, still no answer, and he cursed. "For fuck's sake, Barry, where are you?" Staring at the screen, he quickly typed, *Answer the fucking phone!* before shoving it back into his pocket.

Shaking his head with frustration, he turned his attention back to the group of armed men surrounding him. They were in varied states of dress, from khaki tactical pants and shirts to boxer shorts and flip-flops. They spoke excitedly in Arabic, weapons in one hand, gesticulating at the sky with their spare hands while Khalid, the more senior of the group, listened and nodded. Noticing Liam watching them, he raised a hand, quietening them down and then spoke in English.

"Sir, we need to move you."

"Move? Why? This is my home."

"I know, sir, but now they know where you are." He raised an eyebrow at the hovering drone. "They're watching us, and we don't know what they'll do next."

"So you want me to run and hide?" Liam spluttered indignantly.

Khalid took a breath before continuing, "If they come here, there's a limit to what we can do. You're paying us to keep you safe and it will be difficult here." He gestured toward the neighbouring properties. "We're surrounded by civilians. Civilians have eyes and ears. The last thing any of us need is a situation that attracts the cops." At this, all the other men exchanged glances and nodded.

Liam grimaced. He'd already lost one home, forced to flee in the middle of the night, and he had no desire to go through that again. He glanced over at the house, locking eyes with Joy, and sighed. But he didn't want to put them in danger, either. Turning back, he asked, "So, what do you suggest?"

"I know a place. It belongs to a client of mine, in the mountains here. It's isolated and easy to defend. I suggest we go there."

Liam still didn't like it. "For how long? You're saying I should hide there indefinitely?"

Khalid beamed, his teeth gleaming white against his jet black beard. "Not at all." He glanced up at the sky. "We'll let these people find us and lure them into a trap."

For the first time in days, Liam felt hopeful.

66

Max swapped out the batteries on the drone, keeping himself busy and trying not to let what he had seen get him down.

"What are you going to do?" Ramesh was still connected by phone, making sure the footage was recorded.

"I don't know yet."

He'd counted five men, all armed with assault rifles. Hakim hadn't been able to supply him with more weapons, so all he had was the Glock 17 he'd taken from Barry, with fourteen rounds in the magazine, and a knife. The property was in a residential area and surrounded by an eight-foot-high wall with only one access point. At first glance, it seemed hopeless, but Max knew from experience that there was always a way. He just had to find it.

He launched the drone again, sending it back toward the villa, while plugging the used batteries into the Nissan's cigarette lighter port to recharge. Thankfully, Ramesh had thought ahead and provided him with three sets of batteries. As long as he kept the engine running, he could almost keep the drone in the air indefinitely.

The route to the villa was saved, so it didn't require any input from Max. He placed the phone and controller in the trunk and stood up, twisting the top off a plastic bottle and gulping down the tepid, artificial-tasting water. As he shifted his weight from one leg to the other, twisting his hips and stretching his calves, he surveyed his surroundings. He was parked in an empty patch of land about two kilometers north of Liam's villa, well off the road. The nearest property was half a kilometer away—far enough that no one would hear the drone or figure out what he was doing.

In his earbuds, he could hear Ramesh's breathing and the sound of typing. Max unwrapped a protein bar and took a bite. He hadn't eaten a proper meal since leaving Dubai the night before, and his stomach growled as he swallowed the first bite.

A soft breeze blew across the land, setting a spiral of dust whirling across the sandy ground. It was now late morning, and the breeze did nothing to cool the air. Max finished the protein bar, screwed up the wrapper, and tossed it into the back of the Patrol. He glanced down at the screen, checking on the drone's progress, then unzipped his pants and peed into the dirt, the liquid drying almost as soon as it hit the ground. He stepped back under the shade from the tailgate and sat down just as an alert on the screen of his phone announced the drone's arrival at its location.

"It's reached," came confirmation in his ear.

"I know."

This time he directed the drone to the neighbouring properties, flying along their boundaries, looking for a way to use them to his advantage. The property on the southern boundary was another villa similar to Liam's, but slightly smaller and with a garden that lacked the maintenance of Liam's. He dropped the drone lower and immediately spotted movement as from around the corner of the villa raced two Alsatians, their attention on the drone above them. They jumped and barked, prompting a man to exit the house and look at what had got their attention. He frowned up at the drone, with his hands on his hips, clearly puzzled.

"Guard dogs," said Ramesh, stating the obvious. Max ignored him and adjusted the controller, moving the drone higher and away from the property, turning it west, avoiding flying over Liam's property.

The property on the western boundary was taller, three stories high, with a flat roof that housed solar panels and a large water tank. In an ideal situation, he could access the roof and, with a silenced rifle, take out the guards one by one. But all he had was a Glock, and the distance to the guards seemed to be at the extreme range of the handgun's effectiveness. He exhaled in frustration.

On the bright side, there were no guard dogs, and the wall facing the road was low. However, the wall bordering Liam's property was still eight feet high and topped with broken glass. Things weren't looking promising. Lowering the drone's altitude, he studied the wall. He'd need something to help him climb it—maybe a stepladder—and once on top, he'd have to deal with the broken glass. A thick canvas draped over the top might do the trick. He could pick up a stepladder and a canvas sheet from a hardware store. He could go in at night, just like he had done on The Palm.

Spinning the drone around, he examined the building's facade. There were sensor lights mounted on each corner. He'd need to enter without triggering them, disable the lights, climb the wall, throw the canvas over the glass, and drop into Liam's compound—all without being seen by the five armed guards. Max grimaced. There had to be a better way.

He directed the drone back into a high hover over Liam's property, pulled his feet up and sat sideways in the rear of the Nissan, his back against the side of the vehicle, and thought about what to do.

"They've moved the Toyota."

Max nodded. Ramesh was right. The Toyota was backed up against the staff quarters, its tailgate open. Max dropped the drone's height. The G-Wagen had also been moved, its hood just visible poking out from the garage.

Max saw one of the man exit the staff quarters, a large kit bag in his hand and after a quick glance up into the sky, dumped the bag into the rear of the Land Cruiser before going back inside.

"What are they doing?" Ramesh asked.

Max frowned. He wasn't sure, but it looked like they were preparing to leave.

67

"Can you see it?"

"One sec," came the reply from the rear of the Land Cruiser, where Faisal was lying across the bags, peering out the back window with a pair of binoculars. "Yes, it's there, about a hundred metres back."

"Good," Khalid nodded with satisfaction. His plan was working. He looked up into the rear-view mirror and caught the eye of a clearly unhappy Liam Mulroney. "Don't worry, sir, it's all under control."

Liam scowled and turned to look out the window. Khalid watched him for a moment before turning his attention back to the road. He wasn't taking Liam Mulroney's poor attitude personally. He'd seen it before. These rich powerful men were used to getting their own way, used to being in control, and whenever something like this happened, they didn't know how to handle it. But all Khalid could do was the job he was employed for and that was to protect the unhappy man in the back seat. He glanced over at Hassan sitting in the passenger seat, his Glock unholstered and resting in his lap. Khalid hadn't worked with the ex-

Egyptian special forces soldier before, but the El-Sa'Ka Force had an excellent reputation, and the man looked fit and alert as did his colleague Youssef driving behind in the G-Wagen. "Tell him not to fall back too far. We want to make it easy for them to follow us."

Hassan nodded and muttered instructions into his handheld radio.

Khalid looked up into the rear-view mirror and watched the G-Wagen close up. As he looked away, he caught sight of Liam glaring at him again.

"Sir, still nothing from Barry?"

Liam shook his head.

Khalid nodded and turned back to the highway. They were heading southwest along Route 13, a smooth, straight, six-lane road cutting through the vast desert. Traffic was light, and though the speed limit allowed for more, Khalid kept well below it to make it easier for the drone to keep up.

His thoughts drifted to his employer and who might be after him. He had worked with Barry a few years back, providing muscle for a meeting in Algeria. He'd gotten along well with the big Irishman, and they'd developed a mutual respect in the short time they worked together. That's why it seemed odd that Barry wasn't responding to Liam Mulroney's calls. Khalid had even tried calling Barry himself when Liam wasn't around, but got no answer to either the call or the text he sent. He hadn't mentioned it to Liam, but his gut told him Barry was no longer in the picture.

Glancing in the rearview mirror, Khalid saw Liam staring out the side window, his mouth set in a tight line, deep furrows on his forehead. He looked exhausted, with bloodshot eyes and several days' stubble on his jaw. Khalid knew Liam was involved in something illegal—he'd seen the kind of men Barry met with in Algeria. But his job was to protect, not judge the morality of those who hired him. If someone needed Khalid's services, they clearly weren't working for Mother Teresa. With his eyes on the road ahead, he asked, "Still no idea who it is?"

There was no answer, and he looked up into the mirror. Liam was paying him no attention.

"Sir?"

Again there was no reply, and Khalid glanced over at Hassan, who stuck out his lip and shrugged.

Oh well, Khalid thought. They were being paid well, and they had already received the first half of their fee, so there was no reason to complain. His team was well-trained and well-armed. With the plan he had in mind, they would take care of Liam Mulroney's enemy quickly and be back to collect the second half of the payment in no time.

68

"Tell me what you're seeing, Ramesh." Max had left the monitoring of the video feed to Ramesh, preferring to keep his eyes on the road.

"They're continuing along Route 13, both in the middle lane, I guess about a kilometre ahead of you."

"Okay. And you're sure the drone will continue to follow them?"

"Yes. It has an active tracking feature which, once it locks onto a target, it will continue following it. It's really clever, it...."

"For how long?" Max interrupted, not interested in a scientific explanation.

"For as long as the battery lasts, which...oh."

Max frowned. "Oh, what?"

"There's about another ten minutes before you need to swap batteries."

"Shit. I could lose them." Max thought fast. So far, everything had been going well. With the drone, he had watched the vehicles leave the compound, and Ramesh had activated the tracking feature, leaving Max free to follow behind at a safe distance. They had been driving for almost forty minutes, at first heading west out of Muscat and then turning southwest along Route 13 across the desert plains toward Nakhl. He glanced down at his fuel gauge. "I'm going to need some fuel soon, too. Shit!"

He could hear Ramesh furiously typing, then his voice, "There's a service station five kilometres ahead. You can swap the batteries out and refuel at the same time."

"But how will I find them again?"

Again he heard rapid typing.

"There's no exit for the next fifteen kilometres. As soon as you change the batteries, send it up in the air again. They'll have to be on the highway. It's got a range of fifteen kilometres, so it will find them."

"Speed, what about speed? Will it catch them?"

"Seventy-five kilometres per hour. At the moment you're doing seventy."

Max grimaced. "It won't work. By the time it's flown back to me, I've swapped the batteries out, and sent it up again, it won't catch them."

He heard typing, then a sigh. "Yeah, I think you're right."

Max exhaled loudly and drummed his fingers on the dashboard. All he could do was reduce the downtime and hope by chance the drone could catch up. He pressed down on the accelerator. "I'm going to get closer. See if you can find out where they are heading."

69

K halid spotted the sign for the service station and slowed, indicating right and pulling into the right lane. "Tell Youssef we're stopping for five minutes."

"Why?" Liam asked from the rear seat.

Khalid looked up into the mirror. "I need a leak." He heard Liam mutter something unintelligible, but ignored him. He didn't need a leak. They had only been travelling for forty-five minutes. But he suspected the drone would soon run out of juice and would be unable to follow them. Most drones averaged thirty-five to forty minutes of flying time, and he guessed whoever was tracking them would need to change the batteries. The easier he made it for them to track him, the better.

"Can you still see it?"

"Yes," replied Faisal from the rear. "Still about a hundred metres back."

"Good." Khalid took the exit and pulled into the service station forecourt and pulled up beside the petrol pump. He glanced over at Hassan. "Tell Youssef to top up the tank. If anyone needs the toilet, go now. We leave in five."

Hassan began speaking into the radio as Khalid reached for the door handle.

"I've lost it," Faisal called out from the back. "It was there, but it's just disappeared."

Khalid hesitated. He hoped he was right about the batteries. "They'll be back," he muttered, then opened the door and stepped out. He ducked his head back in the car and caught Liam's eye. "Stay inside, sir. Faisal will watch over you."

J ust two kilometres back, Max screeched to a halt on the hard shoulder, grabbed the controller from the passenger seat, opened the door, and jumped out. He ran round the back of the Nissan and opened the rear tail-gate and grabbed the fresh batteries, then stood back and checked the controller. It was close. He stared up at the sky, and a moment later he saw it, the tiny dark shape of the drone, like an insect against the glare of the sky than it grew larger dropping as it narrowed the distance before settling on the hard shoulder beside the car. Max bent down, picked it up, pulled the spent batteries from the body, and immediately replaced them with the fresh batteries. "I'm launching it again," he said and heard Ramesh's acknowledgement in his earbud. He stood back, launched the drone, then, with the controller, sent it back toward the service station. The entire process had taken less than two minutes. He set the drone to its maximum speed and watched the screen, ignoring the rush and occasional honk from the passing traffic. Less than two minutes later, the service station came into view on the screen and he heard Ramesh's excited voice in his ear.

"They're still there."

Max breathed a sigh of relief. He closed the tailgate and moved back round to the front of the Nissan and climbed in. He stared at the image on the screen. Both vehicles were being filled up, and he saw one man returning from what he assumed to be the rest room. He kept the drone in a high hover above the forecourt and waited for the vehicles to pull out.

"Any idea where they might head, Ramesh? I'm not sure we'll get this lucky twice in a row."

"This highway ends at the border with the UAE, but they could turn off anywhere. There are small towns all along the route."

Max looked up from the screen and gazed out the window. To his right, the Jiddat Al Harasis Plateau spread flat and wide as far as the eye could see. To his left, the desert spread out flat until it reached the foothills of the Western Hajar mountains, the stark rugged peaks rising high above the desert floor. Where could they be going? He doubted they would head back to the UAE, so it had to be somewhere in Oman.

"They're moving again," Ramesh's voice brought him back to the present. He glanced down at the controller in his lap and watched the two vehicles pull slowly out of the service station and head toward the motorway.

Max locked the drone onto the lead Land Cruiser, then put the Nissan in gear and pulled out onto the highway.

70

"Tell me more about where we're going," Liam demanded, his eyes fixed on the man driving the Land Cruiser. The rage he'd felt when he first saw the drone above his property had settled into a gnawing irritation. As if it wasn't bad enough that someone was trying to take over his empire, now he was taking orders from a stranger and had no idea where they were headed.

The men had shown up at Barry's request. Barry had assured him he'd worked with them before and trusted them. Normally, that would've been enough for Liam—he trusted Barry with his life. But now, after not hearing from Barry for two days, Liam was having doubts.

What if Barry had betrayed him? What if he'd sold Liam out to his attacker, and these men were taking him into the desert to get rid of him? But then, who was flying the drone? The whole situation was confusing, and Liam hated being in the dark.

Khalid looked up into the mirror. "It's a *Qasr al-saqr*. Do you know what that it?"

"No, of course I fucking don't." Liam snapped. "Do I look like I would know?"

Khalid's eyes held his for a moment before returning to the road. "It's a falconry lodge in the foothills of the Hajar mountains. A client of mine owns it."

"A client?" Liam wanted specifics.

Again Khalid looked up into the mirror. "Yes, a client. A man I've worked for in the past."

"Details. I want details," Liam snapped.

Khalid sighed. "He's a Prince. A Saudi Prince. That's all I can say. He likes to come here with his birds."

"And he's happy with you using the place?" Liam sneered.

"He doesn't know."

"Huh," Liam scoffed and looked out the window. He should have stayed back in his villa.

"Mr Mulroney, with respect, my duty is to protect you, and that's what we'll do. I have a reputation for keeping my clients safe, a reputation I have no intention of losing."

Liam turned back to look at Khalid. "You'd better. I'm paying you well enough."

Khalid nodded, taking a deep breath as his shoulders rose and fell. "The lodge is isolated and easy to defend. If anyone hears gunshots, they'll assume the Prince is in residence, practicing with his hunting rifles. I know the caretaker—he'll let us in. A generous contribution to his family's well-being will guarantee his cooperation," he glanced into the mirror, "and his silence."

"Hmmm."

"You will be very comfortable. The lodge is, how can I say... furnished in a standard befitting a member of the Saudi Royal Family. You'll have everything you will need, and *inshallah*, you'll be back safe and sound in your villa within a couple of days."

"Inshallah," Liam failed to hide the scepticism in his tone.

Khalid looked sideways at Hassan before replying. "Everything is God's will, Mr Mulroney."

71

T he Nissan Patrol was parked off the road at the edge of a village, nestled in the shade of a cluster of date palms. Max crouched beside an old stone culvert that ran through the trees and into a terraced vegetable field, refilling his water bottle. The water, crystal clear and cool, flowed down from a mountain spring, teeming with tiny fish that swam around his bottle and nibbled at his fingers. Though the foothills were cooler than the plains below, it was still warm, and the sun beat down harshly on any exposed skin outside the shade.

Max was still dressed in the black clothes from the night before—not ideal for the desert heat. But after refueling at the service station, he had picked up a brown *masar* and wrapped it around his head in the Omani style, shielding himself from the relentless sun. He stood up, took a swig of the cool spring water, and looked around. A donkey, tied to one of the date palms, glanced at him curiously before turning back to the pile of straw it was chewing. A mynah hopped across the donkey's back, pecking for ticks, then squawked and flew away.

The terraced vegetable fields, green and thriving with onions and tomatoes, stretched out below him, framed by ancient stone walls that had been there for hundreds if not thousands of years. In the distance, he could hear voices from the village, but no one was outside — the locals were smart enough to avoid the midday heat. The scene was peaceful, almost timeless, and if it weren't for the Nissan Patrol parked nearby, it could have been a scene from centuries ago.

The drone was back in the rear of the Nissan. It wasn't needed right now. Max knew exactly where they were.

About two kilometers from the village, a private road branched off from the main route, winding three kilometers up into the mountains to a luxury hunting lodge, reportedly owned by a minor Saudi royal. Ramesh had done his homework, digging up ownership records and even finding photos from an architecture magazine feature. Max had studied them, as well as taking a high-altitude drone flight over the area. He understood why the men had chosen this location.

The road climbed toward a hilltop where the stone-built lodge sat, offering 360-degree views through its large glass windows. It was isolated, far enough from any nearby habitation that gunfire would go unnoticed. The lodge overlooked rocky slopes with almost no cover, making it easy to spot anyone approaching. Behind the lodge, the land dropped into a dry *wadi* before rising again, towering over 2,500 meters to the peaks of the Al Hajar Range. It was a stunning location—ideal for a prince seeking a luxurious wilderness retreat and a bit of falconry. It was also the perfect vantage point to spot anyone approaching.

He was facing five heavily armed men in a building with

clear lines of fire in every direction. All he had was a Glock 17 and a diving knife.

He took another gulp of the clear mountain water, swallowed, then tipped his head back and poured the rest over his face, washing away the dust from nearly twenty-four hours of nonstop travel. Stepping out of the shade, he faced the sun, letting its warmth dry his skin. He took a deep breath, feeling the tension and worry drain from his body. There was no point in stressing anymore—he hadn't come this far just to stop now. He was on a mission, and he would see it through to the end. If he didn't succeed, at least he'd know he gave it his best. But that was a thought for later.

Walking back to the parked Nissan, he pulled out the floor mats and laid them down at the base of a date palm. Sitting down, he unwound the *masar* from his head, balled the cloth into a pillow, closed his eyes, and within minutes was fast asleep.

72

L iam had to admit, the view was stunning. Below the window lay a stone terrace, and beyond that, the ground sloped steadily down toward the plains. The landscape was dry and rocky, with patches of sand and clusters of date palms scattered throughout. The minerals in the rocks painted the slopes with colors—the dark grey of basalt, the reddish-brown of sandstone, purple iron-oxide, and streaks of white limestone. In stark contrast was the green of the date palms stood out, and in the distance, he could see the white and sand-colored buildings of the nearest village, surrounded by the vibrant green of irrigated vegetable fields.

But he wasn't here to admire the view.

Reaching into his pocket, Liam pulled out his phone and stared at the screen. Still no call or message from Barry. Even worse, there was no phone signal. "For fuck's sake," he muttered under his breath. Turning away from the window, he glanced around the expansive, open-plan living room. A massive U-shaped leather sofa faced the stunning view, with a highly polished onyx coffee table in the center. Behind the sofa hung an almost life-size portrait of an Arab man, likely in his forties, dressed in a crisp white *thobe* and a red-and-white-checked *shemagh,* held in place by a black *agal.* A hooded falcon perched on the man's arm.

Liam sniffed and continued to survey the room. The decor surprised him. When he'd heard the owner was a Saudi prince, he had expected white marble, chandeliers, and gilt-edged furniture. But the lodge was simple and tastefully furnished—the real highlight was the view. Apart from its size, he had seen fancier villas in Dubai. There wasn't even a television on the wall.

He walked away from the window, across the rough stone floor, and out through the heavy wooden double doors to the central entrance hall. A corridor ran off to the left and right, leading either to the bedrooms or the service areas. The front door was open and one of the men walked through carrying a large canvas duffel bag. He nodded at Liam and turned to walk down the corridor.

"Where's Khalid?" Liam called out, and the man jerked his head toward the front door.

Liam walked across the Persian rug that covered the floor of the entrance and stepped outside. Both vehicles were backed up to the door, their tailgates open, the men unloading and Khalid was standing off to one side having a conversation with the elderly caretaker. Spotting Liam, he nodded and called out. "We'll be done soon, sir."

"There's no phone signal." Liam grumbled.

"No, sir. We're off grid."

"No internet either?"

Khalid said something to the caretaker in Arabic, gave him a pat on the shoulder, then walked closer to Liam. "No internet, sir. The owner uses this place as an escape from the modern world. Just him, a few close friends, and his falcons."

"Huh, a fancy escape."

Khalid shrugged.

"How long do we have to stay here?"

"As long as it takes, sir." Khalid put his hands on his hips and looked up into the sky. "It shouldn't be long, though. Youssef spotted the drone overhead earlier." Looking back at Liam, he said, "I think they'll make their move soon."

Liam sighed, his eyes on Hassan, who slung an assault rifle over one shoulder and hefted a heavy bag onto the other. "Okay," he replied reluctantly.

"Make yourself comfortable, sir. You're in the primary suite. I'm sure you'll find it to your liking. One of the men will make something to eat soon."

"Good, I'm starving...and thirsty. Where's the bar?"

A shadow passed briefly across Khalid's face.

"There's no bar, sir. Alcohol is *haram* in our culture. But I'm sure you know that."

Liam sneered. "London is full of your princes, drinking in nightclubs and shagging prostitutes. Don't give me that *haram* nonsense."

Khalid remained silent, the only indication he'd heard being a slight twitch of his right eye.

Liam scowled at him for a moment longer, then turned and walked back into the house. "Bloody rag heads," he muttered under his breath. The sooner this was over, the better. At least in Dubai, he could get a drink.

73

The drop in temperature woke Max. He blinked, momentarily disoriented, before the memory of where he was came flooding back. Sitting up, he stretched his neck and then pushed himself to his feet. The sun was low on the horizon, casting long shadows across the desert floor. The donkey was gone, its owner must have come while Max slept. He was surprised he hadn't heard anything—he must have been more exhausted than he realized.

He grabbed his water bottle, refilled it from the culvert, and gulped it down before checking his watch. An hour until sundown. Still time. He returned the floor mats to the Nissan and re-wrapped the *masar* around his head. From a distance, he could easily pass for an Omani, and with night falling and his fluent Arabic, he didn't foresee any problems.

Sitting on the tailgate, he checked his phone. There were three missed calls from Ramesh and a text message from a UK number.

He smiled at the text message but returned Ramesh's call first.

"Where have you been?" Ramesh asked excitedly.

"Sleeping."

"Sleeping? How can you sleep at a time like this?"

"Huh," Max chuckled. "Experience. Sleep when you can, wherever you can."

"Hmmm," Ramesh didn't sound convinced. "Well, while you were sleeping, I've been doing some more research. An Omani architect based in Muscat designed the lodge. I found the plans they had registered with the Ministry of Housing and Planning. I'm forwarding them to you now."

Max's phone buzzed with the incoming message.

"Thank you, I'll take a look."

"The property is completely off-grid. Solar powered, well water, no telephone or internet."

Max nodded thoughtfully. That suited him. No-one could call for help. "Good."

"What are you going to do?"

"I don't know yet. But you'll either hear from me or you won't."

"Oh." There was a long silence then, "I ah... I... I hope I hear from you."

Max nodded, as if Ramesh could see him. "So do I, Ramesh. So do I." He ended the call and stared blankly at the phone in his hand. What he had said was true—there were no guarantees in life. He would do his best, and hopefully, it would be enough. But at least he was on the right path. Shifting his focus back to the phone screen, he ignored Ramesh's plans and tapped on the message from the UK number.

Nicola.

His cheeks twitched into a smile. They had known each other for such a short time, but the intensity of it made it feel like a lifetime.

As the message opened, his smile widened. It was a photo of Nicola—a selfie—standing in front of a class of preschoolers. She looked much happier than the last time they'd met, more rested and relaxed. His heart skipped a beat, feeling something in his chest that he hadn't experienced in a long time. He zoomed in on the photo, enlarging it until her face filled the screen. Those striking emerald green eyes he remembered so well. Her thick brown hair tied back in a loose ponytail, highlighting her sharp cheekbones. He grinned, thinking back to the first time he'd seen her—her and her friend Tracy, scared and distressed at the Mangalore airport. That moment had set him on this new path, this new life, offering him a chance at redemption. A chance to make up for all the things that haunted his dreams and churned his gut with guilt.

He took a deep breath, a renewed sense of determination filling him. He would see this through. He would bring down Liam Mulroney's evil empire—for Nicola, for Tracy, and for all the victims of his destructive trade.

74

K halid checked the selector switch was set to safe, then inserted the thirty-round magazine into his freshly cleaned M4. He gave it a gentle tug to ensure it was locked in place, then pulled the charging handle to the rear and chambered a round.

Looking up, he noticed Liam Mulroney watching from the sofa, a sullen expression on his face. He was probably still sulking about not getting a drink. Khalid gave him a polite smile that didn't reach his eyes. "I suggest you get an early night. Get some sleep while you can."

"You think they'll attack tonight?"

Khalid pushed back his chair and stood up. He looked down at his weapons lying on the bedsheet he had spread across the dining table to protect the wood. "I'm counting on it." He picked up his Glock 17 and slipped it into the holster strapped to his right thigh, then slung the M4 over his shoulder. On his left hip was a 7 inch Ka-Bar combat knife and in each side pocket of his tactical pants were two more thirty-round magazines. He caught Liam's eye again. "Please stay away from the window and keep the lights to a mini-

mum." He jerked his head toward one of the other Saudis
who was sitting at the opposite end of the dining table
cleaning his weapon. "Salman will be inside with you."

Liam Mulroney nodded and Khalid studied him for a
moment before nodding at Salman and making his way to
the door. The sun had set an hour ago, but there was still a
trace of light on the horizon. He stepped outside and eased
the heavy entrance door closed behind him. The silhouette
of a man standing in the driveway shifted slightly at the
noise and raised a hand. Khalid walked over.

"All clear?"

"Sākit mithl al-qabr," came the reply. "Silent like the
grave."

Khalid chuckled and placed a hand on the man's shoulder. "Let's make sure it's not ours."

Hassan grunted and turned his attention back to the
long entrance road that wound away from the lodge into the
valley. Khalid continued to be impressed with both him and
Youssef. Both men were in their late thirties, but had kept
themselves lean and fit. He'd watched them clean their
weapons and prepare their equipment, and they did so with
the same attention to detail Khalid expected of anyone who
worked for him.

Khalid took a deep breath of fresh mountain air and
slowly turned to look at the surroundings. The lodge was
built on a false plateau, the top of the hill levelled to provide
a flat platform for the construction of the lodge. The
building was at the forward edge of the plateau, making
most of the view, while at the rear was the parking, the caretaker's quarters, and the access road.

Khalid had sent the caretaker away for the night. He
wanted no witnesses or, indeed, any collateral damage.
Since leaving the Saudi Armed Forces and starting his secu-

rity firm, he'd built up a sturdy reputation for reliability and professionalism, qualities he'd carried over from his previous career. He believed in discipline and professionalism, even when working for clients with a less than palatable reputation. He wanted to ensure there were no civilian casualties, and if there was any damage to the lodge, he'd make sure it was repaired from the hefty expenses bill he would send Liam Mulroney when it was all over.

Stepping away from Hassan, he began walking around the edge of the parking, skirting the two parked vehicles toward the southern corner of the lodge. He pressed a button on his radio and murmured, "This is Alpha. Coms Check. Bravo, check in, over."

"Alpha, this is Bravo," replied Salman from inside the lodge. "Loud and clear, over."

Khalid continued, receiving replies from the other men as he made his way around the lodge, patrolling the stone-flagged terrace at the foot of the windows. He passed Youssef at the southern corner, then made his way along the western side of the lodge, scanning the dark slope and listening for any signs of movement. Faisal was stationed at the northern corner, while Salman was resting and keeping an eye on Liam for two hours before switching with Hassan. The guards would rotate every two hours. It was going to be a long night, but each man would get two hours of rest and rotate positions to prevent complacency.

Khalid paused halfway along the western boundary, peering into the darkness. His eyes had adjusted, but the ground sloping away from the lodge remained a murky expanse of black and grey shadows. The faint light from the moon did little to illuminate the area, and he cursed inwardly for not bringing night vision gear. Still, they were well-armed and held the high ground, and he doubted anyone could approach the rocky slope without being heard. If an attack came, it would likely be by vehicle along the entrance road, and Hassan would spot them in time to react.

He tilted his head back, gazing up at the sky and marveling at the vast expanse above. The sight filled him with awe, as it always did. *"Subhan Allah,"* he whispered. "Glory be to God." He sighed contentedly. There was no fear in him—he was doing what he was trained for. His life's length was in God's hands, and he felt at peace.

———

75

Max adjusted his binoculars and watched as a man appeared, silhouetted against the windows of the lodge. The shape of an assault rifle was clearly visible at the man's side. He stopped for a moment, looking out over the slope.

Max had been sitting in a small gap between two boulders for nearly thirty minutes. He estimated he was just under six hundred meters from the lodge, well out of earshot and hidden by the darkness in his black clothing. Unfortunately, he didn't have night vision equipment, but the faint glow from the lodge's internal lights provided just enough illumination to make out the sentries. One on each corner, plus the one patrolling. Max figured there was at least one or two more—likely one at the entrance and perhaps another inside, either resting or watching Liam Mulroney. That's what he would do, though he would have made sure all the internal lights were off. But he suspected the man in charge of security had to compromise to keep his client happy. Liam Mulroney probably wasn't too keen on sitting alone in the dark in a stranger's lodge halfway up a mountainside.

Max watched as the patrolling guard continued toward the northern corner, spoke briefly with the other guard, then disappeared from view. Lowering his binoculars, Max took a moment to assess his situation.

Max was armed with a Glock 17, with only fourteen rounds left in the magazine. Strapped to his leg was the diving knife that had last seen action outside Liam's villa in Dubai. In the backpack at his feet, he had the drone and its controller. Dressed entirely in black, he had smeared mud from the culvert over his face and hands for extra camouflage. He was alone and under-armed, but had to make do with what he had.

Moving as quietly as possible, he unzipped the backpack and carefully pulled out the drone, setting it on a flat patch of ground beside the boulder. He was no longer in contact with Ramesh—there was no phone signal once he left the village—but he could still fly the drone. The controller connected to the drone via radio frequency, not reliant on a cellular signal, which was fortunate given what Max had planned.

Glancing at the luminous dial of his G-Shock, he noted the time. It was 7:30 in the evening. He still had plenty of time. Slowly, leaving the drone behind, he began crawling on his belly, away from the lodge and down the slope.

76

L iam couldn't settle. He'd sat for a while on the massive sofa under the watchful eyes of Salman, watching the sunset and the moonrise. Under different circumstances, he could have appreciated the beauty of the lodge and its expansive view, but he wasn't in the mood to enjoy anything. After a while, when the view turned to a black expanse punctuated only by the occasional passing figure of the guards, he got up and began roaming the house.

Salman stayed where he was. He had finished cleaning his weapons and was now sharpening an evil-looking knife in slow, rhythmic strokes on a whetstone. He hadn't spoken a word since Khalid left, and Liam wasn't sure if he could even speak English.

Liam wandered into the kitchen and flicked on the light. It was a professional setup, with stainless steel countertops and industrial-looking appliances. He opened a few cupboards, more out of boredom than hunger, but found nothing ready to eat. The double-door refrigerator offered little beyond bottles of sparkling water and diet soda. He cursed under his breath and shook his head. Of all the princes he could've ended up with, it had to be one who strictly observed his religion, even outside the country.

Sighing, he let the fridge door swing shut, then leaned against the stainless steel counter. In a way, he almost hoped an attack would come tonight—it would at least be over and done with, and he could get back to his normal life. He was confident that whoever was coming wouldn't last five minutes against the men Barry had lined up. They were far more professional than the men he'd lost in Dubai—fit and battle-hardened, unlike his men who had grown soft living in the big city.

Barry. Liam grimaced. What had happened to him? Surely he hadn't double-crossed him. There had to be a reasonable explanation for why Barry hadn't been in touch. Liam pulled his phone from his pocket and glanced at the screen. Still no signal. He cursed again. No booze and no phone signal. What kind of Saudi prince was this guy?

Even if Barry wanted to reach out, there was no way to contact him while Liam was stuck in this lodge. He took a deep breath and exhaled slowly. If he was being honest, he missed Barry more than his own brother, Caim. Caim, despite being blood, had always been a thorn in his side, an irritation he had only tolerated because they were family. But Barry? Barry had been more of a brother than Caim ever was. They'd been through so much together, the good and the bad, and Liam missed his steady presence, his wise counsel. Without Barry, he doubted he could have built his empire to the success it was.

If only he were here now. "Where are you, Barry?" he whispered into the empty kitchen, the only response being the hum of the refrigerator. He heard footsteps and looked up to see Salman appear in the doorway. He reached in and switched off the overhead lights. "No more lights," he growled.

Liam shrugged. So he did speak English...of sorts.

77

I t had taken Max over three hours to crawl into position on the eastern side of the lodge, on the slope just below the entrance road.

His elbows and knees were bruised and tender from the rocky ground and the palms of his hands rubbed raw. He'd done something similar before, in the southern part of the Golan Heights. His unit had been tasked with ambushing an ISIS linked militia rumoured to be infiltrating into Israel from Syria. He and his team had taken the entire night to get into position before laying up for three days waiting for an attack that never came. But then he'd had NVGs, knee and elbow pads, and a drone on constant over watch. Here it had been solely up to him and he'd made sure that every movement was slow and measured. It appeared to have worked as so far there were no signs he had been spotted by the men in the lodge. Once in position, he had rested, hydrated, and watched the sentry pattern. They rotated the guards every two hours. He'd observed three rotations and was now, at just before two am, almost at the end of the fourth rotation.

Max wanted the guard at the entrance gate just above him to be bored and ready for a change. Judging by his body language, that was already happening. When he had taken over this position he had stood in the middle of the road, alert, constantly scanning from one side of the road to the other, but now he leaned back against the low wall, his weapon hanging beside him on its sling and from the faint sound Max could hear, appeared to be singing to himself.

Max slid his sleeve back and checked his watch. One fifty am. It was time. He turned on the drone controller and activated the drone. The low light camera provided enough of a picture for Max to navigate and he sent it up into the air until it was level with the lodge, then flew it closer. He saw a shape move on the terrace in front of the lodge. The drone had been spotted.

There was the crackle of a radio above him, and he heard the muttered voice of the guard. Max looked away from the screen, toward the entrance, where the guard was now standing with his back to him, looking toward the lodge. Max directed the drone in a sudden dart to the north, then changed direction and swooped back to the southern corner. He heard a shout, then another figure appeared on the screen beside the first. He flew the drone closer and buzzed the heads of the two guards, who ducked and shouted.

Looking away from the screen of the controller, Max again checked on the position of the guard above him. He was still facing the lodge and talking into his radio. Max slowly got to his feet, put the drone in a hover about five metres back from the lodge at head height, then began making his way up toward the lodge entrance.

He was halfway up when he heard three sharp cracks. Instinctively, he dropped to one knee, but something told him the shots weren't aimed at him. The sound was different—he'd been shot at enough times to know. Glancing down at the controller in his hand, he saw one of the guards attempting to shoot the drone. Max quickly moved the drone higher and further back, shifting it sideways just as another three shots rang out. He needed to act fast—they wouldn't miss for long. Rising swiftly, he continued up the slope, confident the guard above him was distracted.

Reaching the low wall, Max placed the controller on the ground and stepped out onto the roadway, unsheathing his knife. In two quick strides, he was behind the guard. He grabbed the man's head with his right hand, clamping his hand over the guard's mouth while simultaneously plunging the knife into his neck with his left. The guard let out a muffled gasp as Max drove the blade forward and away, severing his larynx and carotid artery. Warm, sticky blood coated Max's hand as the guard went limp, collapsing back against him.

Max caught the guard's weight and quickly dragged him behind the wall, lowering him to the ground. He could still hear gunfire and the shouts of the men at the lodge, but the drone had done its job. Wiping the knife clean on the guard's clothing, Max slid it back into its sheath. He relieved the guard of his assault rifle, slinging it over his shoulder, and pocketed the two magazines he found. Swapping the partially used magazine in his Glock for a full one from the guard, he knelt down and checked his watch. Less than two minutes had passed.

His heart raced as adrenaline surged through his veins. He took a deep breath, exhaled slowly, then repeated the process to steady himself. Another shot rang out, followed

by an excited shout. Max glanced at the drone controller—
its screen had gone blank. They'd hit it.

Just then, a voice crackled over the guard's radio. Max
removed it from the guard's belt and held it to his ear.

"Alpha calling Foxtrot. Can you hear me, over?" a voice
asked in Arabic.

Max frowned. Who was Foxtrot? Was it the guard he'd
just killed?

"Alpha calling Foxtrot, over."

It had to be him. The other guards would have
answered. Max held his sleeve over the microphone,
muffling his voice and replied in the same language, "Alpha,
this is Foxtrot, loud and clear, over."

"Anything on your side? Over."

"All clear, over."

"Good. Stay vigilant. I'm sending Delta to join you.
Double shifts from now on, over."

"Copy, over."

Max stood and looked down at the dead guard who was
dressed similarly to him, in a dark shirt and tactical pants,
and they were about the same height. In the dark, Max
might just be able to pass for him. He unwound the *masar*
from his head and replaced it with the dead man's checked
shemagh, wrapping it around his head and face. Then, after
unsheathing his knife once more, he stepped back onto the
road and waited for the man with the callsign "Delta."

78

L iam jolted awake, lying fully clothed on top of the massive bed in the master suite. He hadn't realized he'd fallen asleep, but something had startled him awake, and judging by his racing heart, it wasn't good.

Bang, bang, bang.

There it was again—gunshots. Panic seized him, and he rolled off the bed, hitting the floor hard. His heart pounded, adrenaline surging through his veins. They were under attack again.

He heard shouting in Arabic, followed by more gunfire. Flattening himself against the floor, he pressed up against the side of the bed, struggling to control his breath.

He heard rapid footsteps, boots on a stone floor and then a voice, "Sir?"

"Over here," Liam called out, suddenly embarrassed to be lying on the floor.

The footsteps came closer and then he heard the voice again. "Good, stay down." Liam turned his head and saw Faisal by the window, back against the wall, holding his M4 at the ready.

"Are we being attacked?" Liam asked, his voice shaky.

"We're not sure yet, sir. But don't worry, I'm here."

Faisal's calm confidence went some way toward easing Liam's panic. He rolled over and sat up, sliding his back against the wall. Outside, the gunfire continued, mixed with shouting, and then a distant cheer. Faisal's radio crackled to life. He listened, nodded, and muttered a reply.

"What's happening?" Liam demanded.

"The drone, sir. We destroyed it."

"The drone?" Liam blinked, confused. "They sent it again?"

"Yes, but—" Faisal's radio crackled again. He listened, replied quickly, then stepped away from the wall. "Sir, stay here. Lock the door. Don't let anyone in except us. Understand?"

"Where are you going?" Panic surged in Liam's chest. "You're leaving me?"

Faisal made a calming gesture with his hand. "Don't worry, sir. You're safe. We just need extra eyes outside, just in case."

Liam opened his mouth but couldn't find the words. He watched Faisal move toward the doorway.

"Lock the door, sir," Faisal called back before disappearing down the dark corridor.

"Fuck!" Liam cursed, scrambling on his hands and knees across the floor to the door. He shut it quickly, locking it with trembling fingers. Then he scurried back to the corner of the room, pressing his back against the wall. His breaths came in short, panicked gasps, his hands shaking uncontrollably.

"Fuck it," he muttered, feeling the fear clawing through his body—ashamed of it, but unable to stop it.

79

Max heard the lodge door creak open and steadied himself. He half-turned, raising a hand in acknowledgment to the approaching guard, then shifted back, feigning focus on the road. He didn't want to give the guard a clear view of his face.

He slowed his breathing down, and extended his awareness out behind him, listening to the footsteps, the scuff of clothing and the faint metallic clink of a weapon as it brushed against something. He estimated where the guard was, based on the sounds, and guessed how long it would take him to reach him.

The M4 he had taken from the dead guard rested loosely across his body, his left hand gripping it lightly. In his right hand was the diving knife, held in a firm but relaxed grip.

Max took another slow breath, closing his eyes so all his awareness went to his ears. The footsteps were closer, but still not close enough.

"Have you seen anything?" the guard called out in a low voice.

Max shook his head. *"La,"* he replied, without turning around. "No."

The guard was getting closer but then suddenly the footsteps stopped and Max heard something else.

It was instinct more than anything else that saved Max. Max dropped low, twisting as he swept his leg out, connecting hard with the guard's ankle. The guard's M4 jerked upward as he stumbled, and a shot fired into the air.

Something had made the guard suspicious, but Max didn't have time to think about it. He had dropped the M4 but still had the knife in his hand and he lunged forward, plunging it into the man's thigh. The guard screamed and staggered back, firing two more wild shots into the darkness.

Max twisted the knife, ripping it free, then slashed across the back of the guard's knee, severing tendons. The guard collapsed. Max pounced, stabbing again and again, anywhere he could reach. The guard thrashed, desperately trying to aim his weapon, but Max was relentless.

Somewhere in the back of Max's consciousness he was aware of shouting but his focus was on the man in front of him. He needed to kill him and kill him fast now he had lost the element of surprise.

A boot struck Max's chest, knocking the wind out of him, but he pressed forward, blocking another blow with his arm. He brought the knife down, sinking it into the guard's gut repeatedly. The man screamed, lashing out with fists and feet, but his movements were slowing. Max took a blow to the head, his vision bursting with stars, but he didn't stop. He climbed on top of the guard and, with one final thrust, buried the knife in his throat.

Blood sprayed across Max's face, and the guard went still.

Shouts echoed in the distance, followed by gunfire. A

bullet whizzed past Max's head, forcing him to roll off the dead man, leaving the knife jutting from his throat. He scrambled toward the wall as more rounds cracked through the air. One ricocheted off the stone, another tugged at his pants.

Just as he reached the corner for cover, he spotted the sling of the fallen M4 near his feet. Max snatched it up and dove into the darkness, disappearing from sight as gunfire continued to rain down around him.

80

I t was the sound of a dying man that got to him.

At first there was gunfire, but then the bloodcurdling screams of a man fighting for his life.

When his home had been attacked before, it had happened so fast he hadn't had time to think. Barry had been with him, taking control, protecting him, returning fire. The thought of death had not even entered his mind, just an indignation that someone dared to violate his home.

Now it was different. So many had died in such a short space of time that the reality of his own death felt like a looming certainty.

His body shook uncontrollably, and a sudden warmth spread through his groin. He'd lost control of his bladder. Panic clawed at him. He couldn't stay here. He wasn't going to die alone, helpless, without at least trying something. Anything.

Fighting through the terror and the betrayal of his body, he pushed himself onto his knees and crawled toward the door. The screams had stopped—cut short with a choking, gurgling sound—but the shouting and gunfire continued, now coming from a different direction. How many attackers were there??

He raised a shaking hand to the lock, hesitated for a second, then unlocked it and tugged down on the door handle. The door cracked open, and he gulped down his fear before peering through the gap. The corridor was empty.

Biting his lip, he looked back over his shoulder at the sprawling, opulent bedroom. No, he couldn't stay here. They would find him soon enough. He had to move.

Gripping the handle, he pulled himself to his feet, his legs trembling and feeling like they belonged to someone else. His breaths came in rapid, shallow bursts as he whispered, "Holy Mary, Mother of God, please protect me," before staggering unsteadily out into the corridor.

81

Rounds whistled overhead, ricocheting off rocks and sending stone chips flying into the air. Max was confident they couldn't see him, but he wasn't about to take any chances. He stayed low, catching his breath and assessing the damage to his body.

The fall had knocked the wind out of him, and sharp pain shot through his already bruised ribs. But he hadn't let it stop him—adrenaline and the instinct for survival pushed him forward, putting as much distance as he could between himself and the lodge.

He waited for the gunfire to die down. They were shooting blindly into the dark, wasting ammunition. Eventually, they'd figure that out. Once the adrenaline wore off, they'd stop firing and reassess.

Sure enough, he heard a shouted command, and the gunfire ceased.

Slowly, he turned his head, making sure he was out of sight, then adjusted his position, pressing his back against the boulder, shielding him from the lodge. He flexed his fingers and began methodically checking his body for injuries. His right elbow throbbed, worse now than when he'd first approached the lodge, the result of slamming it against a rock during his dive behind the wall. His right rib cage was tender—one rib in particular sent a spike of pain through him when he touched it. Cracked, maybe even broken. He inhaled slowly, testing his lung capacity until the pain forced him to stop. Not ideal, but manageable. His stomach was bruised from the boot he'd taken, but his legs and face seemed unscathed—at least no worse than they had been after his run-in with Barry.

His knife was gone, but it didn't matter anymore. Stealth was no longer an option; he didn't need silence now.

Thankfully, despite his frantic scramble across the rocky slope, he still had the M4. He guessed there were about twenty-five rounds left in the magazine, plus the two extra mags he'd taken from the first guard. That gave him roughly eighty-five rounds. Plus the Glock. He reached behind him to check for the handgun, but there was nothing there.

"Shit," he muttered. He must have lost it in the fall. He took a slow breath, wincing as his rib flared in protest. Eighty-five rounds for three men. The odds were looking better than when he started.

He also had their radio. He pulled it from his pocket and ran his fingers over it in the dark, checking for damage. It seemed fine. He turned the volume down and held it to his ear. Silence.

Max leaned his head back against the rock, thinking through what the guards would be doing. Right now, they were likely grouped together, expecting an attack from the road. They'd be communicating verbally for now. But soon, they'd spread out—each taking a different side of the lodge —and that's when they'd need the radio.

They wouldn't find the first guard's body until daylight,

so they wouldn't know Max had one of their radios. They wouldn't risk driving away just yet either, fearing an ambush on the road. Their best bet was to hold their position at the lodge, use the high ground, and wait for daylight.

Max checked his watch. It was two fifteen a.m. He had just under four hours to finish this.

82

K halid crouched behind the wall, his eyes locked on the dark outline of Faisal's lifeless body sprawled on the driveway.

Faisal had been a good man. They'd served together, and when Khalid left the military to start his private security business, Faisal had been one of the first to join him. Khalid, a bachelor, had spent many evenings as a guest in Faisal's home in Riyadh, enjoying the warmth and generosity of his friend and his wife, Huda. The thought of breaking the news to her filled him with dread.

If he survived long enough to do so.

Whoever they were up against was no ordinary adversary. Faisal had been a strong man, an ex-paratrooper who kept himself in peak condition, but there he lay, life snuffed out by an unseen attacker. Hassan was gone, too. The ex-*El-Sa'Ka* soldier had known how to handle himself, and yet both men had been taken down in a matter of minutes.

Youssef and Salman were on either side of him, still firing blindly into the night, but Khalid knew it was futile.

There had been no return fire, their attackers disciplined enough to save their bullets and keep their position hidden.

Khalid took a deep breath, trying to steady his nerves. They needed to take control of the situation.

His gaze lingered on Faisal's body once more, and he whispered, "*Inna Lillahi wa inna ilayhi raji'un.* Indeed, we belong to Allah, and indeed to Him we will return." Then, turning back to the task at hand, he reached out and touched Salman's leg. "Stop shooting. It's pointless."

Salman grunted in response, lowering his weapon and sliding down beside Khalid. Youssef, realizing he was the only one still firing, glanced over and followed suit, dropping behind the wall.

83

Max stayed hidden for a long time, unwilling to reveal his position. The gunfire had stopped long ago, and the desert had returned to silence. Nothing moved, not even the wind. Above him, a satellite streaked across the starry sky, the only sign of movement in the stillness.

He listened to the guards' radio chatter, but they kept their communication brief. The three remaining men simply checking in, reporting no activity.

After a while, Max risked a look. He peered around the boulder toward the lodge entrance. No one stood in the road now, but he assumed at least one guard had to be there, using the wall for cover.

To test his theory, Max felt around and found a rock about the size of a baseball. He leaned out slightly and threw it as far to the left as he could. As the rock sailed through the air, he quickly glanced back toward the lodge. A moment later, the rock clattered to a stop, bouncing off other stones. A muzzle flash appeared near the right side of the entrance, followed by two quick shots. There was a guard behind the wall. Max heard excited chatter on the radio, the guard probably calling for reinforcements. That gave Max an idea.

He needed another way in—charging up the road wasn't an option. He felt around for more rocks and grabbed two. Crouching low, he threw the first rock to his left and immediately transferred the second rock to his right hand, throwing it down the slope at an angle.

After about thirty minutes of crawling, Max had nearly circled to the western side of the lodge when he heard a faint sound. He froze, holding his breath, straining to listen. Had he imagined it? The ringing in his ears from the earlier gunfire made it hard to tell, but the desert was so quiet that he could almost hear his own heartbeat.

He waited, motionless, but heard nothing more. Just as he was about to move again, there it was—a faint noise, like a stone being kicked loose. He tensed, scanning his surroundings. Was it an animal?

Then came the unmistakable sound: the scuff of a shoe on stone.

Someone was moving out there.

84

The sound came from ahead, but diagonally above Max, closer to the lodge. He slowly raised himself onto his hands, peering between the rocks. It was too dark to see anything clearly unless it moved, so he waited, his breathing steady and quiet. His eyes scanned the slope until he saw it—a shadow moving downhill.

Max dropped back to the ground. It had to be one of the guards, trying to outflank the attackers while the two others kept them busy at the gate. He thought for a moment. They would likely maintain radio silence until the guard got behind their targets. If Max could take him out quietly, it might be a while before anyone realized he was missing. He regretted losing his knife and the suppressed Glock. He would have to do it the hard way.

He wedged the M4 between two boulders, memorizing the shape of the rocks so he could find them again in the darkness. Once more, he slowly raised his upper body, scanning the slope. Now that he knew what to look for, he spotted the man easily. He was closer now, and at his current pace, would pass Max within five meters. Max decided to wait until the guard was past, then take him from behind.

He lowered himself and listened to the man's approach. The guard was trying to be quiet, but was moving too quickly for the rough terrain. Max could hear his breathing —short, rapid breaths. The man was tense, his breathing out of control. Fear had taken over. Max knew that feeling well. It didn't matter how seasoned a soldier was—once the bullets started flying, composure often went out the window. But Max wasn't like that anymore. His training in the ashram had taught him to master his fight-or-flight response, keeping him calm but alert. His breathing was slow and deliberate, in through his nostrils, out through his mouth, his heart rate steady.

The guard was nearly on top of him now, but Max waited, resisting the urge to move too soon. Only when the footsteps had passed did he raise himself slightly and look. The man was five meters downhill, unaware. It was time for Max to make his move.

He rose silently to his feet and followed.

85

L iam crouched by the front door, peering through the glass panel as the guards fired over the wall. He had to find another way out. Crawling backward to the safety of the corridor, he stood and hurried toward the kitchen. There had to be a service entrance. No prince, no matter how 'minimalist' he claimed to be, would let staff use the front door.

He remembered a door in the back of the kitchen. Once there, he crossed the room and opened it, glancing inside. It was dark, and he didn't want to risk turning on the light. A row of red LEDs blinked in the shadows, and he reached out, feeling his way along the wall, his fingers brushing against the machines—washing machines and tumble dryers. "Off grid," he muttered. "Bullshit." But a laundry had to lead outside. He felt along the wall at the far end and found a door.

The handle was locked, but after fumbling underneath, his fingers found the latch. He pulled it back and pushed the handle down. The door creaked open, and a cool air brushed his face. Liam froze, listening to the distant gunfire at the front of the lodge. Hearing nothing from this side, he took a deep breath, opened the door wider, and stepped out.

It was dimly lit outside, and he could see a row of washing lines within a fenced compound. He moved along the fence, his fingers tracing the rough surface, searching for an exit. Finally, he found a gate in the far corner. The simple latch clicked softly as he raised it, but as the gate swung open, the hinges squealed in protest. Liam froze, his breath caught in his throat, and waited. But after a minute it appeared he had got away with it, so he slipped through the gate and looked around.

He was at the far edge of the terrace that wrapped around the lodge. The ground dropped away into darkness, but off in the distance, he could see the faint glow of village lights. If he could make it there, maybe he could steal a car and get away.

Edging forward, he found the end of the terrace and crouched, lowering himself over the edge onto the slope. The jumble of rocks and stones underfoot was barely visible in the dim light, and he knew he would have to move carefully to avoid injury—or worse, being spotted. But he could do it. He was Liam Mulroney. Putting aside the shame of earlier in the night, and feeling more confident now he was moving, he stepped out into the darkness.

86

The man had no situational awareness, which worked in Max's favor. As he crept closer, he focused on his footing, ensuring each step was silent. He got within two meters before deciding to rush him. Halfway there, Max's foot dislodged a rock. The man froze, but before he could turn, Max was already on top of him.

They hit the ground hard, the man gasping as the wind was knocked from his lungs. Max, grateful for the body cushioning his fall, kept his weight on him. He grabbed the man's head with both hands, yanked it back, and slammed it into the rocky ground beneath them. There was a sickening crunch, followed by a groan of pain and a struggle for breath. Max pulled the man's head back again, then paused. Unlike the guards, this man was clean-shaven.

Realizing who it was, Max shifted his weight and turned the man over. Grabbing his shirt, he dragged him into the faint light thrown by the rocks and peered at his face.

There was just enough light to confirm his suspicion despite the blood and smashed nose.

Liam Mulroney.

Liam wasn't fighting back, still gasping for air. Max let go of his shirt, shoving him back to the ground before quickly patting him down for weapons. He found nothing but a cell phone and a wallet, which he tossed aside. He grabbed Liam's shirt again, yanked him into a sitting position, and leaned in close.

"Liam Mulroney," Max whispered.

Liam's eyes darted in panic, his breathing labored. Blood streamed from his nose, dripping into his mouth. He coughed, spat the blood out, and finally met Max's eyes.

"Who sent you?" Liam gasped.

"No one," Max replied, keeping one eye on the lodge above. The guards hadn't noticed yet.

"Then who are you?" Liam rasped, his voice shaky.

Max stared at the broken man. A week ago, Liam had been a powerful businessman, arrogant in his success, running a business that ruined lives for his own luxury. Now, he was nothing.

"I'm the man putting an end to your business."

Liam gulped, his eyes wild with fear. "But why? We can talk... I have money. Let's negotiate."

Max exhaled slowly. "I don't want your money. I want you to stop selling drugs."

"I'll stop!" Liam coughed, spitting more blood. "I have enough money. I can give you some."

Max shook his head. "You'll never stop."

"I will. I swear it."

Max stayed silent.

Liam's voice cracked. "You... you killed my brother?"

Max nodded.

"Are you going to kill me?"

Max glanced up the slope at the lodge, then sighed. The

image of Liam Mulroney—the ruthless drug lord—had driven him forward. But now, with Liam broken and sniveling before him, he looked pathetic.

Max released him, shoving him flat on the ground, and stood. He lingered for a moment as Liam whispered, "Thank you, thank you. I promise, I'll stop."

Without a word, Max turned away, staring toward the horizon. He had to move before the sun rose.

87

K halid stood on the terrace, gazing out over the desert as the sky slowly lightened with the rising sun. Normally, a sight like this would fill him with awe, but today, all he felt was a deep sense of failure. He'd lost two men—one of them a dear friend—and now his client was missing. His M4 hung on its sling as he rubbed his face, pinching the bridge of his nose. Exhaustion settled deep into his bones. They had been awake all night, constantly on edge, anticipating an attack from any direction.

After hearing movement near the entrance that didn't lead to anything, the three of them had stretched themselves thin, patrolling the lodge's perimeter, always alert. As dawn neared, they'd allowed themselves to relax slightly. No one, they thought, would attack in broad daylight.

The lack of a follow-up attack had confused Khalid. It wasn't until he finally went inside to check on their client that the truth hit him—hard. The noise at the entrance had been a diversion. While their attention was drawn away, another team had slipped in through the laundry and taken Liam Mulroney right out from under their noses.

Khalid grimaced. He had been foolish, complacent. He had trusted their elevated position and superior firepower, but the enemy had moved like ghosts, quiet and invisible. Fortunately, there was no damage to the lodge that he would need to explain to the owner.

Now, both Youssef and Salman were scanning the landscape with binoculars, looking for any sign of their missing client or his captors. Khalid sighed, turning back toward the lodge. He didn't think they would find anything, and he had something equally important to do. Now that daylight had come, and the threat seemed to have passed, it was time to give his fallen comrades—Hassan and his friend Faisal—the dignity they deserved.

An hour later, Salman's voice crackled over the radio. "*Afwan ra'ees.* Excuse me, boss. I think I've found something."

Khalid straightened up with a heavy sigh and released the hosepipe he'd been using to wash the blood off the driveway. He took one last look at the two bodies he had rolled in blankets and moved into the shade near the front door before making his way to the terrace.

Both Salman and Youssef were waiting for him. When Khalid arrived, Salman pointed to the sky. Three large birds circled high above—vultures.

"Over there, sir," Salman said, pointing down the slope. He handed Khalid a pair of binoculars.

Khalid adjusted them to his eyes and focused in the direction Salman had indicated. It took a moment, but then he saw it. A leg poking out from behind a rock.

A sense of dread settled in Khalid's gut. He handed the binoculars back and climbed down from the terrace, heading toward the slope. "Keep watch," he called over his shoulder. "They might still be around."

It took him only ten minutes to reach the body.

Khalid stood over it, hands on his hips. He couldn't see the face; the head had been crushed under a large boulder, but he recognised the clothing.

He let out a heavy sigh and looked up at the sky. The vultures circled closer, now four of them, waiting for him to leave. Glancing back down at the body, he prayed for the third time that day, "*Inna Lillahi wa inna ilayhi raji'un.* Indeed, we belong to Allah, and indeed to Him we will return."

88

TWO WEEKS LATER

Max stepped forward, pulling his friend into a strong embrace. He held him tight for a long moment, then patted him on the back and pushed him gently to arm's length. "Thank you, Azar. You're a good man. I couldn't have done this without you."

Azar swallowed hard, too emotional to speak.

"With your help, Azar, we've made the world a little better. Don't ever forget that."

Azar smiled through his tears and nodded.

Max bent down to grab his bag. Azar finally found his voice. "Will you come back to Dubai, Max?"

Max shrugged. "I don't know, my friend." He gave Azar's shoulder a firm squeeze. "But if I do, you'll be the first person I call."

"Even before Ramesh?"

"Even before Ramesh," Max chuckled. "Now I've gotta go, or I'll miss my flight."

Azar nodded again, wiping his eyes with the back of his hand.

Max turned and walked toward the departure hall. As

the automatic doors slid open, he glanced back. Azar stood by the curb, his taxi behind him, waving a hand in farewell. Max returned the wave, adjusted the bag on his shoulder, and stepped inside.

He was traveling light, with just the bag over his shoulder, and had already checked in online. Heading straight for immigration, he tried to shake off the nervous tension creeping in. His passport was genuine—although gained illegally from a corrupt British consulate official before being officially issued under his new identity. It had gotten him into Dubai, and he hoped it would get him out just as smoothly. But, after everything he had done, all the crimes he'd committed over the past few weeks, it would be ironic if a passport was what brought him down.

The line moved forward slowly, and to distract himself, Max thought back over recent events. His body had healed nicely, the bruises mostly faded, with only a slight twinge of pain when he took a deep breath. He was clean-shaven now, his hair neatly trimmed, and he looked like a smart international traveler in a linen shirt and pants.

Max's only contact with Colonel Hakim since leaving the lodge had been a single text: *It's done.* He'd discarded the phone immediately after that.

Since then, the newspapers had been full of stories about a major drug bust by the Dubai Police, largely because of the anonymous information Ramesh had provided. Colonel Hakim Al-Hamadi's reputation was soaring as the officer who had taken down an international drug empire..

The incriminating photos and payment records had been erased. Max had done his part; now it was up to Hakim to redeem himself and turn his life around.

Max reached the immigration counter and handed over his passport with a smile. "Good evening."

The official barely glanced at him, quickly flipping through the passport, stamping it, and handing it back.

Max nodded his thanks and walked past, letting out a long breath of relief. Leaving a country was so much easier than entering it. A few steps further, he stopped by the departure screens and looked down at the boarding pass in his hand.

He was heading back to a place he never thought he'd see again.

He checked the flight number on the pass and scanned the screen. There it was, leaving in just under an hour.

Flight IX840 on Air India Express.

Direct to Goa.

ALSO BY MARK DAVID ABBOTT

For a complete list of all my books please visit my website:

www.markdavidabbott.com

The John Hayes Series

Vengeance: John Hayes #1

A Million Reasons: John Hayes #2

A New Beginning: John Hayes #3

No Escape: John Hayes #4

Reprisal: John Hayes #5

Payback: John Hayes #6

The Guru: John Hayes #7

Faith: John Hayes #8

The Neighbour: John Hayes #9

The Chinese Cat: John Hayes #10

The John Hayes Bundles

The John Hayes Thrillers Bundle #1 : Books 1-3

The John Hayes Thrillers Bundle #2 : Books 4-6

The John Hayes Thrillers Bundle #3 : Books 7-9

The Max Jones Series

The Mule: Max Jones #1

The Irishman: Max Jones #2

The Hong Kong Series

Disruption: Hong Kong #1

Conflict: Hong Kong #2

Freedom: Hong Kong #3

The Hong Kong Series Bundle: Books 1-3

The Devil Inside Duology

The Devil Inside

Flipped

The Devil Inside : Bundle

As M D Abbott

Once Upon A Time In Sri Lanka

ABOUT THE AUTHOR

Mark can be found online at:
   www.markdavidabbott.com

on Facebook
   www.facebook.com/markdavidabbottauthor

on Instagram
   www.instagram.com/markdavidabbottauthor

or on email at:
   www.markdavidabbott.com/contact

Milton Keynes UK
Ingram Content Group UK Ltd.
UKHW020934041024
449263UK00011B/528